Eternal

Kiss

A Rhyming Romance Novel

By

Stéphane Parker

Imperative Publishing
Detroit, MI

For more information, email:
ParkerRomance@ParkerRomance.com or Follow @ParkerRomance

©2009 by Stéphane Parker

ISBN 10: 0-615-29485-5
ISBN 13: 978-0-615-29485-8
Library of Congress Control Number: 2009914214
Published by Imperative Publishing, LLC Detroit
Printed in the United States
Book design by Stéphane Parker

ACKNOWLEDGEMENTS

First and foremost I would like to thank God for blessing me with the talent to put words together on paper and in speech in a way that impacts people in a positive manner. Secondly, I would like to thank my parents, Sharon and Carlos Parker, my brother Mike, Aunt Linda, Uncle Rusty, cousins Jeannine, Ashton, and Brian. I would like to give a huge shout out to my home boys Corey Trimble, Jerome Rutledge, Karon Knott, DeAndre Clark, Darryl Holmes, and Damien Moore—y'all told me I got flow and now the whole world will also know. I would also like to give a sincere thank you towards Beans and Bytes cyber café and LaShaun Phoenix Moore; I'm gracious to have met you. Beans and bytes is where I publicly recited my first rhyme, I'll always remember and honor that. Love y'all all—redundant I know, but still so true.

To all of my internet writers and friends: Jenine Hathaway, Rhea Lewis, Ken 'K-SOUL' Masenda, Lauren Mintz, Alan Carter, Dewayne Mitchell, Elizabeth and Carol Minisee, Tami Jackson, Amanda Ramsey, Juliuna Mitchell, Shenee' Davis, Ashley Boyd, Larry Hawkins II, Thu Cao and all Xanganites who dropped me props when I wrote as Genesis X, Authentic Sentence, Authenis X, and Alphaflomegaman during 2004-2007. To all the current Xanga account holders who've prop me while I'm writing as Arrive__Arcane. Thank you for your support and positive words.

And here are all the people that I want to give a shout out to and acknowledge their presence in the world:

My BAQ, Sarah Phinnessee, D'Mara Brooks, Osie Trimble, Neeyn Bland, Michelle Morton, Rodnicka Hill, Mike Will, Ty Pharaoh, Mic Write, Blak, Phenom, Light Shineth, Shana Powell, Ericka 'Epiphany' Foreman, Mrs. Jelks, President Carol Baxter, Tyrone and Chevette Jackson, Eric Jackson, Tia Jackson, Edward Franco, John P. Kiley, Brian Hawkins, Christopher Taylor, Kyra Wilson, Mr. Barwinski, Ms. VanAsh, Mrs. Milstone, Ms. Tyus, Ms. Roberta Rutherford, Mr. Trice, Ms. Daisy Lopez, Shakey Moore, Benjamin Anderson, Napoleon Wright II, DJ Eitan, Brandon Adolph, Brandon Allen, Demarius Clark, Terrell White, Ed Smith, Colette Smith, Antoine Williams, Angelo Williams, Derrick Williams, Mr. Tranumn, Shajuan Gray, Tiffany Giles, Latasha Weaver, CJ Simmons, 'Q', Jayson Cooper, Dr. Softley, Dorian Grahmm, Markus Morrison, Marysia McMillian, Frank and Mary McMillian, Nicole and Naomi Parker, Tera Reed, Keenan Baxter, and Kyle Knott, Alexandria Dye, Jin, Faith-Rachel, Ms. Gebhart, Todd Harris, Pete Ayers, Tim Mamon, IADT staff, Mike Rosik, Damon Christopher, Teresa Mienk, Don Stevens.

It's not intended to be disrespectful if I've missed your name in this acknowledging list. My total recall of all the people I'd like to mention is not fully being activated. My apologies are honest. Thank you again to every mentioned name above. I've learned something from all of you. I love you all.

PREFACE

I've been pondering about being in love and how that "in love" kiss would be. In doing so, I mulled the idea over in my mind until the concept of 'Eternal Kiss' was conceived. Indicating a timeless event, I imagined that this kiss would freeze all time and space while embellishing emotion and sensation exponentially to degrees yet to be identified.

Being in love can manipulate and distort reality and yes, I declare that I've been on the circumference of its threshold. So, courageously, I attempt to convey my interpretation through a rhyming fashion of imagery about an experience I've only come to know through split seconds of pure bliss. Concluding, here is my contribution to the passionate people and all people who love a pair of irresistibly kissable lips. I whole-heartedly thank you. Enjoy my interpretation. Thank you Lord.

I've heard about this book and all I have to say is AMAZING!!! Thank You, this is a breath of fresh air! ~ Jeannine W.

I Read it. You are such the hopeless romantic and literary user...you really get complex with the literary works....metaphors, similes, etc. ~ Jazz

WOW {Fanning myself} Excellent imagery Stéphane ~ Kyra W.

I'm so happy *for* you, and proud *of* you, Ste'phane! Thank you for sharing your words and yourself with me, and everyone else. Our lives are enriched just by knowing you. You wake us *all* up! The dream IS -- and STAYS -- alive! ~ Mary G.

Now that's creative! That's the kind of work I love to read! Very nicely put together and embodies one of the very reasons I write ~ Curtis H.

Beautiful!! I fell in love with poetry all over again ~ Aricka Y.

Visually and verbally appealing. I imagine you could do this all day :] ~ Thu C.

Man, the growth is ridiculous. You do some things that I can only DREAM about doing. It's funny, because we came across each other on Xanga, and the more you were exposed, and the more people commented, I would see some of your style influence their work. I aint playin' you, either. It definitely influenced mine, because I would rarely try to rhyme when I wrote in the past. Now I try to, and it's because of you. Trust, when it comes, when that times comes, Imma let everyone know one of my biggest inspirations is you. All day, everyday, mane. Keep chasin' that dream, grab it by its throat, and make it a reality. Imma keep rootin' for you. ~ Ken M.

You are very talented. It is rare to find someone with a pure passion for words, and I admire you for it. ~ Faith P.

You never disappoint. ~ Ashley B.

I'll give you points for creativity, that's for sure. :) Keep mixing things up, It's always fun to read your stuff. ~ Brandon K.

Always coming up with something new. Very creative. Me likey. ~ Shannon T.

You're as great as you've always been, as great as any has been. ~ Adyre M.

What's nice about your writing is the ability for you to lead us readers through any event! ~ Shelonda J.

Exquisite. Lovely. Enchanting. ~ Tina A.

Man... I LOVED this. "I'm forced to be alright with you because I'm all outta lefts" BRILLIANCE... ABSOLUTE BRILLIANCE. I'm so very impressed right now. ~ Shenee D.

This is well produced and offers something that is hard to find, yet makes you want to seek more. You've certainly out done yourself just as many times before. ~ Chandria D.

You're just effing brilliant. ~ Derrick D.

I love the flow of it. ~ Michelle M.

Now that's passion. I love it. I want to feel like this about someone...have someone to feel it about me. ~ Lauren M.

Yes, sweetie we know you're obsessed. At least you're talented. Some people spend their lives banging their heads against the wall doing stuff they weren't made for. You were made for this. ~ Sharon P.

I like this one. I like the focus on the kiss and how everything comes from that. ~ Benjamin A.

I love the images you use...the words...amazing...you keep getting me excited thinking of how it'll end.....You have me bated breath Mr. ~ Nicole H.

The more I read your writing the more I'm silenced in awe of such beautiful talent. What do I say to this!?!?! Oh my goodness! ~ Cheryl B.

Dang bruh...hot..that's all I can say! ~ DeAndre' C.

I like your use of metaphor, and how you constantly change the meaning of things. It's pretty cool. ~ Carlos P.

Ste'phane, you are absolutely crazy for writing this. You're one who knows how to engage, a mad writer on a rampage and I can't wait to turn the next page. ~ Jinga C.

This story truly held my attention, the flow is dynamic...As with your other writing, you take on this voice that causes one to stop and listen.... Nice. ~ Leandrea H.

Okay, I'm impressed. You make it happen. ~ Mike P.

I was told that we are mortals until the first kiss...
Tonight is going to simply be amazing... I know it

I'm sitting here, imagining your presence in my place
I'm growing anxious and finding it harder and harder to wait

Impatient for your face, I glance out the window and gaze upwards
I control my excitedly jumping nerves by reciting a personal mantra of words

"Be like the river... calm and smooth... be... like... the... river"

Dark blue and pink clouds scatter themselves throughout the vast purple sky
I hear crickets quickly and continuously chirping, it's going to be a hot night

I stand and pace around the house cleaning up and straightening items
As I grab the candles debating if I will light 'em, the anticipation heightens

*Maybe I should light 'em... she'll be here in a minute... Ok, I'll light
'em*

I walk to the kitchen, check dinner, and decide to let it cook a half hour more
I rotate the chilling bottle of wine as I envision what our night has in store

I excitedly await your face and the allurement of your perfume
Thoughts race through my mind and chill my body despite the heat of June

365 days together, committed to you... it's been wonderful

Our one year anniversary is here, it seemed to have come so fast
Tonight, the seconds will be years and we'll never allow the moment to pass

When you finally walk into my house, I promise to show you affection...
From the doorway to the backyard and in my home's every other section

I'm still mesmerizing over the endless beauty of the sky
I admire at how gently and effortlessly the stars lie

Wow... the world is beautiful

I hear your light rapping at the door and I react responsively
Steady visions of us together keep me balanced, my lungs inhale a serene peace

My nervousness leaves

I head for the front door in a straight line, nonstop
I pursue the tapping as again I hear you gently knock

Knock... kn, kn, knock, knock... knock, knock

I peek through the peep hole and see you standing
Your hair subtly blows in the wind while your physique becomes demanding

It states...

Look at my face, look at my body, look at all of this... tonight... I'm all yours... just open the door

You're holding Happy Anniversary balloons and a small black bag
Your small white purse peeks from under your arm and I'm so glad...

You are finally here!

I swing my peering from your earrings to eyes, from your eyes to earrings
Seems like my brain stops working but my eyes notice you and they starting cheering...

"Open the door... open the door"... and so, I confidently open the door

The large brown door swings open, the screen door welcomes your glide inside
Your precious lips spread wide while in my grasp you confide

We embrace

Your scent fills my nose with a terrifically elegant fragrance
I start to think that the putting on of this aphrodisiac was flagrant

You smell so good and your body is so warm

The temperature in the foyer is increasing
I feel your chest and in unison we're breathing

You are my rhythm

We gently release the other and at the other we just stare
I notice your hair and I also notice your sensual dress wear

You are some type of wonderful... I close the door

We walk into the hallway to the dining room as you ask, "What's cooking?"
I answer "Rice pilaf and baked chicken" as I glance at your seductive looking

You have on a soft, powder blue skirt with a matching tank top
Not for one second did my mental giving of thanks stop

Thank you for being so fine... thank you for being so mine

You give me the balloons and then spread another beautiful smile
Though I just saw you last week it seems like it has been such a long while

I accept the gift with gratitude... holding your hand

I lead you into the living room, I show you the pictures that have the wall lined
While you look, I take a quick peek at my wrist watch to notice the time...

It's just about... 10:10pm

You briefly look around the living room to admire the new works of art
Like a ballerina, you gracefully turn around to face me and I feel the spark

You're staring at me, at you, I stare
Our shine pulsates around the room, our sparks flare

I'm like a deer in headlights, I'm stopped stiff
Time slips, everything seems to pause for this

Sounds can't be heard... everything becomes quiet... I feel weird sensations

Without any words being spoken, I can hear your delicate speech
Though you're no longer touching me, I'm still gripped within your hold's reach

Your movements appear to be in slow motion...

You enter into my inviting soul without me blinking
Without hesitation, you make your way into my thinking

You set your purse on the table; you ease close; ... you...

Bring your head up to kiss my chin, then you kiss my neck
You quickly send your lips to my Adam's apple tender flesh

Ummph

You lean back and stand on the tips of your toes
Very easily, your kiss heats me up until I'm totally froze

I see... you're in pecking mood

The sensations I feel are special, the feeling is impeccable
Your lips move over me just like you're a bird and you're pecking food

They move here and kiss me there... over there and kiss me right here

You have rich kisses like your chocolate mouth has been kept in jewels
Molecules race through my body jetting fuel and they're set to cruise

So that...

My brain can stay conscious, so that my brain can stay focused
I'm in a trance-like coma from your passionate aroma and my heart is now open

Angels surveillance your lip's angle, sending the secrets to Infinite Intelligence
My body wets from your appetite and my calm liquid soul is drenched

I seem to be sweating as your fiery lips kiss my mouth

Your tongue sings the most beautiful song that's ever been sung
The way it sways side to side, my pendulum-like mind is swung...

Over a cliff!

I'm quickly falling into your endlessly erotic abyss
I'm lost within your kiss Alice, I'm in a wonderland and you're my atlas

You wonderfully sweep me across worlds with your twirl
Your fingers at my neck's nape make my hairs curl and ideas to swirl

My ideas mix and blend... they blend and mix

A million times within this first kiss I mentally grin
I replay our kiss again and again and again

Seconds slow to hours and I seem to be froze
Millions of visions tumble around my mind like laundry loads

I can see this and all of our kisses in vivid detail... and...

I envision your lips pressed against mine for a lapse of time
Long enough to equal a million, billion laps of Time

You pass breath to me, you pass life to me
This kiss is stirring up memories in my brain from a past life of we

We are the original Lovers

Thoughts as gentle as a spring's wind sweep through my mind
Nostalgic images grow ripe and stem from my mental vine

Everything that we've been through has been called a fantasy
I've battled three headed dragons and beheaded them rapidly

During the wars of the worlds, I was a strategic colonel
I was shooting stars as ammunition from galactic guns just to earn you

We've...

Sailed up and down the river of time being secluded
Draped in veils of pleasantries, and towards memories we've always alluded

We've...

Been thunderous arrows shot across rainbows
Swam through the glittering soups put into pots of gold

We've...

Dropped coins into wishing wells that were as large as Moby Dick
Turned sea serpents into neat servants that will always wait for us to quit

We've...

Carved round tables and authored books for a King
Pranced a lot in Camelot in the types of nights that are made for dreams

In our past lives...

Egypt has seen us and our combination of locking lips
We've left London bubbling with the heat from our French trysts

And...

I remember in ancient Greece when you couldn't wait to see me
When we hugged, that moment was our seizing and that was 69 B.C.

Together... hand in hand...

We've traveled the galaxies rapidly, dicing the cosmos within eye blinks
Sailing Heaven's seas like the 7 seas showering love causing spaced ships to sink

You know what?

This kiss is like a hurricane with the force of a surging train
It's like a having a Certs of flame, it's like opening the curtains to fame

Because...

You are my action movie, my suspenseful, romantic thriller
You are my tongue dancing killer, you are my destiny fulfiller

I compare kissing you to a warm and pleasant breeze
You buckle my knees with a peaceful ease similar to serene seas

Your lips are so, so sweet...

They must be covered with the glaze of a honeyed moon
My heart lights bright as I venture into your historically oral rune

Your love for me will reveal the path to me

The endless mysteries that lie within you kissing me
Is like a praying mantis in Atlantis with Aladdin's lamp whose desire leads to wishing me

Puzzling?... I know

You chill my flesh while simultaneously heating my insides
The invincible summer that reigns in my veins wants to spring forth and collide...

With your mind... with your body... and with your soul to...

Gently fall and then enter into your every ebony pore
Massaging your intuition with attention, your heart will become an unlocked door...

Only opening to me... only opening for me

I want to express to you what your mouth expresses to my soul
I want your spirit and body and I want both under my ingenious control

That's my mission

With my drifting tongue, I manipulate the ripples of our lake
I want you to feel the rushing rivers of sensations roll as my tongue skates

This living room is turning into a coliseum that houses our great clash
I honestly believe that we can hold this kiss until Eternity throws its white flag

But maybe...

I'm going a bit too far while I'm holding on to this star
Too long have I been contained by glass, this butterfly wants out its jar...

So I can soar!

I'm fantastically swept within a gust of lust to the ninth cloud
In solitary confinement with you as my bed lining, I could sleep within a giant crowd

Peacefully... and I always tell people that...

No one could ever possibly deter me from her
She's my fine feline, the cat's meow and I love her purr

And our foundation and palace of love...

Is being built with our tongues madly at work
Melting kisses that are as sweet as syrup help me discover Mrs. Butter's worth

You... are... Priceless!!!

And...

Since I've seen you and met you in this world
I've always known that you'd end up my girl

I knew... from the first day I saw you...

I could hear the passionate throes echo throughout your soul
You were looking for someone to help your future memories become bold

Then... you looked at me

You had a pair of eagle eyes that could pierce through metal hearts
I recognized that you had a pair of wrecking eyes, you tore me apart

You broke down my cool reserve

You didn't walk, you strolled in powerful strides
I watched closely as our attractive vibes vied to collide

I approached you in a confident and calm fashion
The chill of spring's breeze didn't cool the flame of our matching

We shared an inextinguishable flame

I told you that you were beautiful and that you were beyond description
You told me you heard of my muted intentions before your ears could ever listen

Was that odd?

What was said with my body rang louder than the words that were spoken
You gazed into my soul with an intellect that multiplied my intelligence quotient

I became a genius... all because I had seen this...

Woman who was the only reasons my eyes tried to see
Just to absorb your seduction into my lungs is the only reason my nose was meant
to breathe

You are the reason that...

My consciously unconscious brain wants to think
Why my sailing thoughts vowed that they would never sink

You are the reason... that...

My touch wants your hand and why my legs stand
Why I grew into a man and why I promise to do all I can

You made my life come alive... then you spoke... "Hello"

The sound of your voice was an audible elixir
I concentrated on your kisser as I wondered if you were Love's sister...

Passion

You sang sentences from your thoughts that vibrated my inner chords
Each syllable sliced and cut away my apprehension like a samurai sword

9

I asked your name and you beamed back a heavenly smile
Your name echoed within and throughout my soul a many of miles

You said your name was...

Without touching me you held me, even without my ears I'd hear your call
Your pupils taught me lessons of tenderness that were impossible for me to fail or
fall

I seemed to have forgotten about all things... except you

Your voice is a panacea that can heal every spiritual wound
You must make flowers bloom because you heated up my body with a smile as
hot as June

Your name is...

Your charming name is synonymous with beauty
Attractiveness is graciously draped over you like a negligee and truly...

You're pierced with enthusiasm... and...

You surged my hormones like I had touched live wires
You have the softest grace while possessing the hottest fire

Your grace...

Was like warm silk arousing my skin to dance
Your enticing eyes seduced me with each seductive glance

Your making love to my sight only insinuated our future action
You sailed my passion like a captain and added the music to my rapping

As I stared at you... the spring wind subtly breezed again

Your hair smelled like shampoo and your sweet lips attracted me
Your feminine rhythm had easily entrapped me and matter-of-factly...

I was held prisoner in your presence

I fell into the lakes of your soul and fell in love with your mind
I admired your body and longed for our future day of champagne and crying

That would be our wedding day... trading rings... and on that day...

We'll walk on divine rugs and bring the angelic doves to sing
Our eyes will forever gleam while our love is permanently stitched within the eternal seams...

Of a quilt built by the greatest romantic lovers off all time

Your smile spread tenderness and your angelic movements were the signs
Your true intention was to once again return to Earth to turn my life divine

You're my angel... listen... since I've seen you...

I can't imagine the world without us in the same place
I've now found my destination since I've placed faith within fate

I believe in you... I believe in us

I saw that you were the essence of what imagination could create
You entranced my thoughts and manipulated realities to where I'm positive to state...

Dreams dream dreams where the fantasy woman wears your face
Know that our past, present, and future could never, ever be erased

We will always be here to love each other

If I were cryogenically frozen for a million years my love would still burn
It's too solid to urn and I promise for you that I will always and forever yearn

It seems that...

Time speeds up to chase you away from the embrace of my loving arms
I believe it's jealous and even eternity wishes again to possess your charm

Promise to never leave my side because I'll never leave yours
I'll always love you and intimately breathe you; you'll seep and permeate my every pore

I think... maybe... just maybe...

You were born a terrorist or maybe even a kleptomaniac
You leave the mental planes inside my cranium high jacked

You overtly steal my attention without ever even knowing it
You have sexiness woven into your every gesture and motion with no sewing kit

Your name... again... is...

Your charming name is synonymous with beauty
I know the day you left heaven to seek me caused the angels to act unruly

Because once you've been met... no life form wants to see you leave

I've wished for your affection and then received the route to your direction
You're mixed with all elements of pureness, that's the only way to get your type of perfection

You're the truth

You etched an absolute beauty onto the clay tablets of my psyche
You're going to be my wife, see, we'll continuously move at the right speed

I guarantee that

You know how to hold, mold, you know how to console
You co-op control and patch holes in my spirit with bits from your soul

I don't want to question it but, however God had done it...
He made gold shine, diamonds twinkle and somehow you've come from it

How did He do it?

I aspire to be more like your heavenly spirited being
My stage of life was dull until you changed it into a wonderfully passionate scene

And... tonight standing here kissing you...

I realize that I've never tasted anything so authentic or so true
I can't essay enough about the things that I would do for you

Your divine design was not constructed for lust
It was made from and for a pure love and that's I trust...

"Perfected"... will describe us

Your magnetic personality sticks to my refrigerated heart
The places we frequent would be nothing but disintegrated parts...

If the heat between us had any more energetic sparks

I truly hope that you suffer from kleptomania, steal kisses when you can
I've wanted your lips since I've sensed you and I'm glad to become a kidnapped man...

Of... a heavenly beauty

You're a fine, sublime design that's caught in my minds eye
My goal, the sky's pie that's breath taking enough to make Sighs sigh

Awww

Your tongue ventures through my mouth like it's hiking
My own wrestles back like it's fighting and I'm being strung along for kiting...

On the wind drifts of love... on...

An aerial stretch of caress, riding an intimate wave's crest
Resembling a sun setting West, I'm glowing from the zest of our apex

Yet sadly...

I remember in 1849 when your golden tear drops caused a rush
We were out of touch, but since, I've quieted your yearnings to a hush

We're back together... forever... and we won't ever again divide

I've lost all sense of time since our lips have touched
I'm in a quicksand type of kiss and I don't mind to stay stuck

I won't struggle to free myself

The further I sink within your delicate pool of ecstasy
My proficient senses realize that your soul is moving through the flesh of me

It feels wonderful

Our mouths are speaking a language of extreme delight
Our translation is like pure light, transporting us on cosmic flights

And...

I revel in the euphoria and bask in the warmth of elation
I'm shaking in the greatness; you're the Ruler of the Imagine Nation

The seconds of blessings exponentially increase the affection
You tongue tall tales of an unending, hyperbolic love confession...

Embellished to our reality

Your tongue's precise, elliptical motions present spherical miracles
I intuitively know your rhythm and admire that your talent is lyrical

I knew that as soon as our lips for the kiss met, it was kismet
It was a feeling of being sliced with sugar and spice; you should have a kiss set

Since you have a sharp tongue and from our first encounter when I caught wind of your perfume

I knew that your smell and benevolence...
Could have been evidence that you were Heaven's scent...

Manifested...

Into the physical visual of perfectly proportioned ebony coursing...
Without the slightest of forcing, you became my idea of Ms. Fortune

And... I looked up to you

With your intelligent stare and lightly perfumed scent
You made my mind's eye squint, I was trying to figure if you were the slightest hint

That...

There is a higher level we can manifest after the test
After the pecks and before the sex, after we've passed the temptation of flesh

I liked your genuineness, your warmth, the sound of your unheard laugh
I liked the woman you were showing me and that meant I loved your past

*I'm glad you've traveled whatever road you have because that road
has led you to me*

You elevated the perception of my very soul
Since love's written existence, I wanted to dedicate every ode

You deserved at least that much

You shined purely, you were wrapped in glitter, you shimmered
My mind simmered and as time lingered my eyes were like top notch
contenders...

Fighting for a connection with your soul

I knew that I wasn't necessarily being delusional
I knew for sure that your image was more than just an illusion of jewels...

Fitting within a skirt... and

I was a little skittish to flirt but it would have worked my nerves
I had to attempt to word the finest lines that you've ever heard

I remember your smell

The aroma permeating your pores
Made the legs of the ideas that ran around my mind get sore

And...

With the combination of emotions, possibility and desires, we locked eyes
You innovated the invasion, you arrested the development of thoughts, we locked
eyes

You pioneered the absence of fear, you were so fine
You halted time while exalting shine from a sparkling smile that outlined and then
chalked my mind

I knew that... between two metals under the force of magnetism...

Your smile was simply more than attractive
You're the only woman who's made me honest and passive, to get my every
mental receptor active

You were what my dreamy desires have always craved for
You're the reason that the birds wake up early to sing and bathe for

You are just like the sunrise

You were my fantasy materialized and that day I realized
Angels do walk amongst the sinful because you were the clearest sign

And...

In the following months after our meeting, our bond grew stronger, more real
I wanted more of you as you gave me more and more of your vibrations to feel

At that time, March was in season and...

We were full of possibility, ready to spring forward
As we became affectionate, each of our defensive barriers we had up, lowered

March passed

We advanced passed those 31 days and entered into a new month of hope
Enjoying the exclusivity of the events, we stepped through the velvet rope...

Into Relationship's courtyard... April came but...

Rain showers didn't discourage our parade, we could weather any weather
This is when I first noticed our grip was tight as tethers yet as soft as a bed of
feathers

And April went

We were walking and talking more candidly now
My longing for you was increasing; I questioned how much time was allowed?

We had to maximize every second... we had to answer the calling

May became present

You showed me how much love could actually rest in a soul's heart
You slowed the days, exposed my daze, and our nights never seemed dark

May leaves

We spoke of becoming an item, we spoke of the benefits
I felt nostalgic sensations then, I figured we had always been a fit

Then... June was in full swing... it's official

We're an issue that's making heads line and news stand like a circulatory
Everyone wanted to catch a glimpse of our living, breathing romantic story

June melted into the fall... the fall fell into the winter

The first kiss we shared was on Christmas on my carpet next to the fire place
With your lips, you robbed my memory banks of every kiss I had before this day

We were involved in a classic cops and robbers scene

I chased your tongue with an urgent, urging surge
I mouthed a passionate splurge with verve; each word I swerved struck a nerve

This was the first time I experienced the wealth of a loving offering
I was adopting ideas of ways to provide your lips with a pleasant fostering

It was easy for you to lean onto your back since we knelt
As we'd eventually melt, our sexual yearnings knew of no such thing as stealth

The gentle flames of fire crackled...

When I looked into your soul, I saw that it was full of passion
It was like you mesmerized me for hours and I didn't notice the hours passing

Your eyes were as fiery as embers lying within a flame's ebbing tide
They waved signs of seduction that were as wonderful as day dreams of Heaven's
skies

Their look was like a trap that I wished to never escape
Their look was like faith itself, and I knew that this moment was fate

It had to be... things were too right not to be

Your body leaked a language that's not spoken to mortals
I was transported to fantasy; the taste of your kiss was the portal

The mist of pleasures felt from your lips froze me, they released me
You're a two legged pillar of truth, I'm being honest, please believe me

Your smooth tongue complimented my rugged passion
Our connection was matching and then the scene unfolded like a hungry man's napkin...

Quickly!!!

Rubbing what your apparel covered, we shared the kiss of lovers
Kisses had our faces smother as your soft hands melted over my hot body like butter

And...

Everything about tonight reminds me of that first time
Out of all of our kissing, tonight is going to make that seem like our worst time

That first kiss didn't have the multiplicity of possibility

Tonight...

Our kiss has the staggering aptitude to soar us to infinite altitudes

Our first kiss...

Didn't have an endless sensation; it was finite, nothing close to infinity

But tonight...

Our kiss has a cryptic caption embedded with instructions to leave every constellation infused...

With an unpolluted and sinless love that's above all suspicion

Of our kissing,

Archaeologists couldn't dig up reasons for us to stop
Ophthalmologists would be ticked of if for one second if they couldn't see or watch

I know that tonight is just the beginning... and it's destined to get better

You manifest a fantasy from this small and simple loving act
You've gotten my train of thought precisely on your same track

You conduct construction

You leave me astonished and demolished with French kissed bombings
These passionate ponderings pause me like I'm reading a passage full of commas

... ...

I find myself again lost in another thought

I recall playing hide and seek with you when we were in paradise
When I found you is when I first and truly noticed your pair of eyes

They possessed an alluring, magnetic and hypnotic glare
With lightning type looks, even overcast skies knew that it wasn't fair

No one can resist your gaze... I'm jolted by your stare

You restrict my thinking to stray its thoughts from you
You ascend me to Pure Perfection; I wonder is my life through since I'm
reconnected with you

Am I in Heaven? I have to be

I feel that this kiss has released my spirit into the ether
I feel your lips in my atomic matter as I think "I've got to keep her"

We're interconnected through this passionate, linear expression
You burst my excitement and affection into infinite directions

The ambience is transient and I'm floating away
We permeate the daze, the craze; even Speech says "You don't say"

To the naked eye, we seem to pervert gravity
Comets blush since they're intending to see us make love astrally

The voyage is voyeuristic and I truly wonder...

Is it better to give or to receive?
Your kiss is more valuable than all the treasures that were lost at sea

19

Indeed...

You're giving me a gift that I couldn't possibly resist
Coasting on a cosmic river, we sail past celestial monoliths

We see that...

It's covered with hieroglyphic graphics of our kissing classics
Drama knows that without you, my entire existence would turn tragic...

Drastic!... And...

It would be like seeing an illusion yet without the magic
The genes I'd pass down would be lagging, perpetually sagging

But...

You're the reason that I was birthed and lent to Earth
The reason that my heart works; you're the liquid that quenches my thirst

I'm into you just as you are into me, you have my rib
Without your half with my half how could I live?

We were forged as one image then split into two pieces
We'd seek the other until time ceases since our souls have signed leases...

With Flesh... we don't and won't own these bodies

Our spirit's frequency can reach unfathomable heights, its range is endless
We shall outlast this and any other planet until every atmosphere is windless

And if we were to create something better... a better planet...

We'd kiss one another to breathe life into another world
Casting down an universal language of love when our tongue's curl

We'll...

Recreate floating spheres with our hopes and tears
We'd replenish the cosmos with models to let life appear

We'll establish a new race of beings as wonderful as angelic harp strings
Co-creating through procreating, the world will be like our fantastic dreams...

20

Wonderful... and understand that...

Before we were embryos and before the months as a fetus
The universe had already arranged an eternal kiss to greet us

To be honest

These impulses you send vibrate my entity, they go beyond this kiss
You provide the essence of what it means to truly and completely exist

Pure love

I didn't have to die to experience the wealth of Heaven
I take pride in inheriting a never ending cycle of triple 7's

You're my residual richness... Of your lavish lessons...

I've become your affluent student
I now possess a panoramic focus outlined by your prudence

I'm stitched within the fabric of your ardency
The skies that blanket us are embroidered with you and me

We leave a precious signature that's more prestigious than any brand name

There hasn't been one fiber in my body untouched by your lips
You take my imagination on vicarious trips and from your fountain, I sip

The red carpet of my lips await you famous technique

You walk kiss upon kiss on the trail of my tongue and across my mouth
Your kisses sway and groove as smooth as suede shoes on my lipped couch

Keep resting your kisses on me

I'm invigorated by your lip's succulent greatness
Quenched throughout my every inch, your juice is filling yet weightless

And because of that...

We've floated beyond every past and future, enjoying every present
Singing the blues on moons and eating croissants on their crescents

My mind's eye twinkle like little lights with the likes of a star cluster
Staring at the constellations in elation, I can't help but to touch her

Through her mind

I've become a telepathic arachnid with an encompassing extension
I've grown 8 legs to walk you on four simultaneous dates, I've received permission...

Into your psyche

I plant seeds of pleasure into your every neurotic atom
Of our trips over the East, West, North, South, even Locations couldn't map 'em

I've spun a world wide web that only you can maneuver
We originate beginnings that are newer, piercing love through the other like skewers

So stick with me

Angels hit high notes as we orchestrate a choir of fire
Our mouths are becoming one with desire and neither one of us can tire

We don't believe in fatigue or of not giving our all
We've lived and died together making sure every ear has heard our call

We've screamed throughout dreams, reigning as king and queen
Sitting on thrones of poems we have always recited Love's theme

"There is no you or me... there is only an us"

Intertwined with every element throughout every era of time
Our kiss is in all things, in all seasons and in all themes of rhyme

Gravity's force has never been able to keep us held down
Reminiscing our past histories and their effects never lets me frown

Our romantic nature whines as we indulge in a French toast
Our tongues connect instead of glasses and this party, we'll co-host

Tonight, we will chaperone the countless moans
Together, we will make sure that no hand roams alone

We'll also supervise every sigh

We're authoring a book of one kiss that'll last 100 pages
Every phrase of every page will be edited by 100 sages

And our book will be perfectly bound

The true love seekers and believers well be our anxious readers
We'll transmit our radiance to the ones that are ready to be receivers

We'll be intergalactic anchors that will broadcast to the masses
To accurately identify our love you'd need more than telescopic glasses

You'd need...

An extensive vocabulary that can describe the ineffable
A whale-sized back pack that can keep all of your nestled clues

A monumental pencil to take notes on sky wide legal pads
To forget all of the knowledge that you thought you knew you had

Because finally...

You'd just have to live in the harmony of your inner self
Let your intuition blaze and it'll cause your reluctance to melt

Then, like us... you'll be completely free... free to...

Caress the flesh, pass on, and then to console the soul
Mold diamonds from coal and become the shining light for all to behold

We play a leading role for couples at love's every stage
Imagine an infatuation extended into an everlasting phase

And then, like us... that's where you'll be stuck

It's an untamed bewilderment that allows me to be your fool
You blueprint the architecture of a romantic lecture and I'm in school

You create and solve problems of our abstract math to always equal one
I taste me and you or is it you and I, I must have a dyslexic tongue

To further explain my condition

I didn't understand it when the Judge through the book at you
For your serial crimes of my mind, my brain cells is where your time is due

You'll forever sit in my consciousness and use my thoughts as your coaster
With you literally in me, honestly, can I wish you to be any closer?

And... if I can, you know I'll find a way

As our tongues further glide and we feel the shudders stutter by
We slice through the clouds of affection like a hot knife through a buttered sky

Very easily... very, very easily

We ascend past the sins and descend through the trends
We're perfect 10's, twin kissing gems whose beings could never end

We're over time in the realms of a continuous current
We're unlocking an immortal river and swimming in its continuous current...

By using Florida's Keys

You couldn't freeze or stop our fiery eruption with polar caps
We've traversed countless globes being guided by solar maps

We've shot each other seductive glances like stars while on Mars
We drove soul across the cosmos with golf clubs as big as Saturn cars

The goddess of love helped our devotion glow like a necklace as big as Texas
Causing Mercury to run to hurry and deliver our planetary message

"Love conquers all... love conquers all, it's true... love conquers all"

Until my flesh is wrinkled and my casket is bathed with the dirt of a grave
This time will be saved, flavored and savored for those memories that have that
crave

With the desire to...

Acquire that perfected prominent dominance
Paying homage to the bondage that's wrapped around an inexhaustible tolerance

You possess poise and patience with your sadomasochistic kissing
You leave my heart beaten and I'm enduring an endearing whipping

This pain is a good pain though

Your tongue flips like the world's greatest gymnast
With ballerina type eloquence you experiment with elements like a chemist

I'm as high as the voices of angels in Heaven's Heaven with lungs full of helium
You swing open the doors to Fantasy's first floor of its mansion and lead me in

And I see...

Long window drapes as grapes, deep love seats made of crepes
Pillars of strawberry shake and murals that epitomize angel cake

Everything looks so delicious

I pick up the master key that'll open the door to the sweetest of all suites
Up stairs of plums and pears, the music playing is the sound of you kissing me

One, two, three...

I enter through the scores of doors anticipating my reward
The heat that welcomes me invites me to keep moving forward

I'm growing more and more excited, more and more warm
I've reached the source of heat and on the universe it's sworn

That you are...

The most beautiful ensemble of flesh that a soul has ever worn
The quintessential stencil outlining the fact that you're Perfection's norm

Your voluptuousness accentuates that your attraction is effortless

Your kisses speak to my body in an elite language of no words
Your kisses must utter in stutters since they re-rub my every nerve

Over and over... over and over... and then over and over again

I marinate in a serenade that's savvy of your flavorful song
I feel my soul awakening; your touch might as well be the dawn

While still kissing me...

You bring your small hands up to round my lips like a clock
My mouth must be 12 and the winding hour must have reached its top

Because... your lips strike my mouth...

Like bolts of an entrancing lightning

They strike my mouth...

Like fear, yet the terrorizing suspense isn't frightening

Your lips strike my mouth...

Like a bowling ball thrown throughout 10 perfect frames

They strike my mouth...

Like posing pilot models taking off on a runway lane

Your lips strike my mouth...

Like matches that set fires to leave my taste buds blazing

They strike...

Up my mouth like a flirtatious conversation

Your lips strike my mouth...

Like a deal that's worth a trillion dollar contract

They strike my mouth...

Like 90mph pitches that sail pass the bat

They strike...

Like rich oil and I'm enriched with the taste of your Texas Tea

Your lips strike my mouth...

Like the gavel of a picketing judge that's sentencing us to stay free

They strike...

My mouth's hunger with air raid bombs of a nutritious love

They strike my mouth...

With awe, I'm feeling like I've accomplished the goal of life as our lips hug

I'm star struck

You issue great lakes of kisses to me at a passionate pace
My brain tissue soaks up your liquid and the stain reveals your face

Nothing can get you off my mind

Your picture is set; it sits in my every frame of mind
You lodge in its collage yet roam in the lines of my rhymes

Your kiss surges my urges putting me at your total service
My system isn't nervous; it's serving as a getaway gate way that's fervent

And so...

The feelings are impatient and continue to rush
From my head down to my legs, my every muscle is flushed

My loads of tension leave, my anxiety dissipates
With acupuncture like precision you deeply and immeasurably penetrate

Through my every line of defensive skin that my body has

Delving past 7 layers of flesh you enter into my blood stream
The devoted Dean of Love's dream, you stitch me within the Sun's seam

This Kiss Is SCORCHING HOT!!!

No past flame can compare to this type of heat
No past excursion of Mt. Everest can get you this type of peak

I'm at the top of the highest, most fiery zenith available

I feel an inferno that's internal; I'm tattooed by your tender embers
I'm addressed with stamps from France and my licking returns to sender

I have never been stingy with my love

From reality, my eyes shall stay closed
My destiny is just too close and yours, you too hold

Our canvas is painted with colors that are too elaborate for regular eyes
We're just too busy to try; we're falling in love while flying throughout the sky

Cumulus clouds surround us and accumulate to crowds
It's been miles of smiles because we've been graciously allowed...

To be our complete and perfect selves

You take my body's temperature to the highest echelon of degree
I enter Heat's house by stepping through the Sun's screen

I'm burning for more of you

Your tongue is the catalyst that's driving this chemical reaction
Faster and faster, memories come in my mind of our past without even asking

While we were in Russia...

Our kisses polished the other creating such a luscious luster

In Germany...

Our tongue's grasp clasped fast and I often thought that we'd never turn it free

In Rome...

Our tongues were like soothing cyclones, spinning icy hot poems

Taiwan, China, Japan?

There's no way that a kiss like this could've been made by a mortal's hands

And I also remember that...

Before wild animals roamed the Serengeti of Africa, I was after you
Before any sculptor could plaster you, I had already captured you

And you had already captured me

My mind holds your indelible face, we hold an incredible fate
We peacefully sit in a permanent place enjoying an infinite space

Before electrons circled the nucleus of atoms in amoebas
I was to need you, seek you, complete you, and fossilize in concrete too

We've been exclusive... and...

We've always had secret locations to rendezvous
Before form had form and before horizons were beautiful views...

I have loved you

Your mouth, my lips, my mouth, your lips
I quest for more, miss; I'm discovering new worlds with four ships

We share a friendship that's in a perfect kinship
We also navigate a leadership to an imperial relationship

So... how can we not... fall...

Into love like we've lost our balance

Or

Fall into love like a roller skater of no talent

Fall into love...

Like Autumn's leaves into a beautiful heap

Or

Fall off into a loving ecstasy like it's a deep sleep

We can rustle through the others covers into their soul's sheets
We can mold heat into skates and calmly stroll in peace

From coast to coast, we'll leisurely coast
Across the X, Y, and Z axis, we uninterruptedly float

Hand in hand... lip to lip

As we outshine the glare of the sun I think "How many thoughts can come?"
In a galaxy where ounces weigh tons our passion could out weigh all sums

We share a massive connection

You domesticate my wild mouth and my wild lips
You have me tongue tied to a kissing booth and I obediently sit

I'm your seduced servant that's here to assist
In anyway I can, I embellish the mist of this kiss

Your kiss rains with the soft sweetness of melting cotton candy

I'm sprinkled with love by a farming daughter of water
Not irritated but irrigated, I'm soaked in hopes of becoming a martyr

I'll die for this kiss

For representation of this type of kiss and this type of devotion
The greatest agents would not breathe until the ocean no longer motioned

The nutrients of your lips appease more than just my hunger
Throughout the ages your divinity has made the most studious scientists wonder

Is there a God?... but...

Tasting your superb marvelousness, I have no question
You're too complete to lessen, too godlike not to be a blessing

I've become an organ donor since I've given you my heart
My tongue, my lungs, my brain, and my every other essential part

I've given you my soul as well

No bottling company in the universe could can your passionate extract
No stock could gain your interest and even heavenly chiropractors want you back

But... you're mine... forever

Until the entire outer space is out of space
We'll massage our mouth's rim with a molasses-like haste

We'll seize the need, enthralled by our clandestine speech
Our lips gossip of our private vacations without using words to speak

You hold my head like it's a heavy pitcher of elixir
You pour a batter of respect into me and use your tongue as the mixer

My mind is spinning

I feel you locking yourself deeply into the rib cage of my chest
The sentence is set; I will live everyday under cardiac arrest

You're my heart and because of that I attest that you're...

The prerequisite of the intrinsic me
The life blood of my being that flows through my arteries

You're...

The keep-the-doctor away apple of my eye
The why for my try, the resuscitator of my life

You're...

The most colorful fruit to fall from His artistry
The ignition to my existence that's forever starting me

You've corrected my galactic calamities with your simple kiss
You've added an enriching and luxurious lift to my value without risk

You are Ms. Fortune

You arrange melodies from your lips as soft as a rose petaled sea
You unwrap me with rhapsodies until I mimic a boiling kettle of tea...

Whistling loudly to our love's theme

Joyously, my awareness toward an aesthetic world enlarges
I'm fluent in all languages being that I translate your covert jargon

You're a secret chef in an invisible kitchen serving me a surreptitious kiss
I become omniscient and my wishes are for a never-ending dish

Your tongue marches a parade of commitment through the hall of my jaws
Waves of pulsating elation ring throughout my mouth and I hear the call

Hello, yes, I'm here

I answer with promptness, engaging into entrapping conversation
Our dialogue is enticing and crisp while your lips start its tracing

You outline my mouth with a tri-lingual tongue
You speak Spirit, Eternal, and Infinite while pleasing my body numb

I drift within your kiss; I'm becoming the "I" and "S"
You miraculously unfold my brain's wings so that I can fly and stretch

From the ninth cloud to the seventh Heaven
You're the only philanthropist on a scale of 1-10 with a kiss rated an eleven

With dynamic antics you draw out my latent passion
You confidently sail to the middle of my desires like a seasoned captain

The pattern of your charted course leads straight to my heart
The sands of my mind shift to unearth a treasure with your name marked

This is Destiny

Golden glitter announce that you're the decided, designed reaper
No other soul has come this far, you're the findings keeper

You can have all that I have to offer

It's been broadcasted that we're on the heir
Being oblivious to Earthly laws we permeate the particles of air

We're fugitives that have ran throughout the marathons of Time
Placing first, we've come to be known as the definition of fine

Fine *(adj) a. finished; perfected b. superior in quality*

Your tongue rolls like movie reels as I watch your show
The four theaters of my mind capture your motion and glows

The illuminating caption of your action causes normal eyes to squint
The sentences of your statements exaggerate width to unfathomable lengths

My inner voice calls to Mind...

You've never toiled with my mental soil
It's always been fertile, only awaiting your fertilizing oil

You plant kisses to my mind's subconscious gardens...
Rooting a deep belief that even before Genesis our conception was starting

We've traversed to the ends of the galaxy
Only to see that in the end is the beginning and that factually...

Time has no end and that time hasn't even started to begin

We're in everything, interconnected throughout the universe
Your lips dissert a curse, I'm to stay inextricably bound to your worth

You dive and delve into my inner wishing well and swim within my senses
A vault of my most cherished thoughts is raided by a kiss that minces...

Sight...

Into division, so I'm able to see twice as much love

Space...

Into dimensions, I can see the lengths, widths, and heights of the Heavens above

Of my sixth sense and its labyrinths, you leisurely amble
The periphery of my mind is extra sensory as I perceive your candle

I melt like wax as my train of thought switches tracks
The flame flickers like your tongue, causing my inhibitions to collapse

In all seriousness...

I'm delirious from your lisp, penned in a padded room being scribbled
My mouth is being written on by a kiss of ink and I'm becoming crippled

I'm a quadriplegic architect whose lips map spots to assemble and curl
Every two revolutions of my cyclic tongue creates another ten worlds

The receptors that sit on the tip and along the sides of my tongue
Activate all of my ten thousand taste buds and invite then to partake in the fun

Your taste is so enjoyable

Your hands jaunt from my neck upwards toward the top of my skull
Your fingers rub my head and divide my consciousness creating my light lull

I'm dozing off into another wonderful dream

You pierce my frontal lobes, making each inner ear ring
My left and right cerebral hemispheres don't fear this thrilling scene

My thalamus overwhelms with the deluge of stimuli
Your lips cool my hot flashes; your kiss is full of small gems of ice

My mental temples reverberate with your celestial echoes
The exclusive feeling behind this kiss is just too special to let go

Simply because...

These past four trillion seasons I've held onto this singular reason
I exist for you and that won't change until the soul of my soul starts leaving

I don't think that can happen

Ethereal oracles watch as we act out their prophecies
We take emotions to a realer state being that we're two houses of Heaven's
property

I realize that I've been passive, that I've been the captive
I take my hands to your jaw line and switch my authority to active

It's my turn to deliver the shivers

My hands swim through your hair slowly pulling back your scalp
Sprinkling cool pleasure into your psyche like my touch is made of talc

I illustrate a portrait of the exuberant pleasure of a million lips
The colors map out love, giving directions for a wonderful trip

You follow the golden path and fiend for another psychological hit
The picture sets like concrete, solidifying its position to permanently sit...

In your frame of mind

Deep sensations occupy your mental plane as your brain sails
My tongue wheels with loco-motion as I steam ahead on this oral train rail

We twist and turn around the vast textures of our tongue's landscape
Our lips pair up to tango at a romantically grand pace

Our tongues dance freely

My mouth's house is a spacious one room loft
Your erratic, nomadic tongue wanders upon a paradise once lost

And... you bring gifts with you

You unveil a 24 karat kiss and you unfold and unroll it
It's been told throughout the skies of an angel with lips that are golden

And you're her... aren't you?

My fingers trickle down the back of your neck, the length of your back
Resting at the base of your vertebrae, my hands plan their next attack

I strategize how to increase our vibes

My touch's circumspection is strategic in finding its next stop
So with my grasp retreating upward, your defenses further drop

I relish in your taste and revel graciously in your flavor
Your mouth's every section is affection and you're entirely savored

I taste...

Wild blueberries, cherries, apricots, apples, kiwi
This conglomerate of fruit raiding my mouth turns me into seaweed

I'm floating within your ocean

With an entertaining flair, my moist muscle acrobats with adeptness
My dexterous tongue flips lightly as I journey into your wetness

The style of pleasure that coat my kiss is the most expensive couture
The certitude I display through my touch and lips makes one thing for sure...

I'm bestowing a love that's too luminous to be defined as glowing

We stand connected, erected as two pillars of example
Our treasure chests open to allow the input of loving samples that are more than ample

We fill each other up

The greatest orators despise their silver tongue since ours are golden
We're to change courses of history, our simple yet profound power was chosen

If I were to ever lose my mind, your kiss would be my compass
You are my thoughts, so your mouth is the North Star that's firmly fixed...

In my brain

We turn our heads in unison, never breaking our rhythmic pace
I can feel your breath on my cheeks and across my face

My birthstone predetermined that I would be your best friend
God intentionally waited to create the strongest things of Earth until the end

A diamond... and... A woman

You've been strong before fibers could ever form muscles
Before leaves had tree houses, you had eased the struggle

You've enticed my demeanor of ice to impatiently melt
While we were Eskimos in Alaska the heat of Ecuador was felt

Your mouth is an oven that bakes the most delectable cakes

You become my pallet that I sit kiss upon passionate kiss on
My Jasmine that saw me as Aladdin's lamp that she had to wish on

And... your wish is my command

Our tongues swoon and spoon, resembling old tales of the moon
We're a pair of lunatics swept into flight like a witch's broom

With a gentle grace...

I erase your physical eyes from your face
My flushes of touches kiss through your clothes to your waist

Use only your mind's eye to see my movements

Moving from your chin, your jaw, your shoulder and arm
You shudder as your body utters to my kiss "You stutter with such charm"

I respond, "Th, thu, thank, thank you, thank you"

With a lapping impediment, my mouth settles on yours like sediment
I wind my tongue like curiously strong tornados of Altoid peppermint

The chills jet throughout your body and slowly ease your skeleton tense-less
Tantalized to realize, I've activated all of your senses, you are defenseless

I send more shivers throughout your body than cryogenic freezers
My flaming kiss crackles with my minty lips acting as combustible teasers

We're exploding this night into our memories

I envelop your mouth with a honeyed syrup that's past being nectarous
We aspire to heights of delicious fire and no one can get next to us

We're higher than high while being deeper than deep

I submerge within the sensation of every yearning urge
I feel every electron's surge and all of your silent thoughts are heard

I know... and yes, I love you too

I further tilt your head back and delve deeper into your mouth
I enter actions of interaction and I'm not looking to exit out

We hover horizontally as my tongue runs wildly with yours
Like two dolphins in a sea not concerned about the shores...

Our tongues jump endless leaps

They jump...

Into the rewards that we graciously reap

They jump...

Like they're playing hop scotch

They jump...

Like the others tongue is too hot

They jump...

Leaping into the other's pristine springs

They jump...

To hail us as King and Queen

Waving upwards and resembling a double helix
The magic of our kiss wouldn't dare be called a trick

This is Authentic

This is genuine how our unabated passion spins
The realest McCoy of joy, this is where truth begins

Here and now

Our lips are of the rarest, most precious commodity
Being entities of honesty, we police the purest of policy

You get what you give

Lying on a bed of air, my right hand rummages through your draping hair
I scale down silken fabrics of follicles that leave my fingers in a snare

My hands are being massaged by bushels of lustrous locks
My touch harpoons through silky black curtains from the bottom to the top

My whisking stroke lazily glides across your hair roots and forehead
My questing hands deviate from the front to now the sides of your head

My touch ventures in your mind and thoughts in all directions
Wandering through the physics of your psyche I expel affection

I burst with thirst and my thoughts multiply and fly
I become a regal eagle soaring through the skies of your mental eye

Imagine that

I see that from the compatibility of our abilities from our affinity
We encourage our amenity's energy to become as brisk as a winter's breeze

We are one

I love your moist and tender lips pressed against my lips
The temperature of our mouth's kiss makes our tongues blazing whips

Our lungs increase, filled with an air of caress
Our lungs deflate, exhaling an air of caress

Of the sun's shine

We mimic it, blazing in endlessness
We can only be emulated by our own unique tremendousness

Destiny has written our script and directed our moves
Destiny has also chosen when we'd win and when we'd lose

So with that known...

As we walk along a road of a million paths
We trust that our better half will sustain the wind's rough drafts

We kiss one another not knowing exactly where it'll lead
If the other did leave, could a crying whisper recreate our "we"...

Or our...us?

We speak to each other in all dialects from our highest, most inner linguist
Understand that if we stopped loving each other then I'd be finished

If our union were to ever cease...

I'd need morphine and all types of pain killers to heal the hurt
I'd dig up 99 million Earths to uncover a treasure of your worth

I'd...

Choke on a city that was once lost until I swallowed the seas
I'd solve the equations of Bermuda's triangle until pi equaled three

I'd...

Make seconds, minutes, and hours types of liquid just to waste time
I'd rob Memory banks of clues until deaf bill boards no longer signed

I'd...

Resurrect every aborted child and let mummy's wrap them in love

I'd flip the world upside down and let Hollywood's stars fall above

So as I venture back to the future...

I won't lose you so I continue to kiss you forward to the past
You're a multifaceted diamond of flesh as bright as a million watt flash

From the words of scribes to the drums of African tribes
From the intellect of the wise, to the meaning of our lives

Of every language of every chronological period
Of every shape, swirl, and symbol of every pyramid

We were that... and are still that

This is a novelty how our being a novelist can kiss a portrait
Every rotation of our tongues sends us on many short trips

We're deeply engaged in this kiss...

Asteroids could collide and we still wouldn't open our eyes
A thousand total eclipses could never block this son's shine

My kiss's diligence lights you up like a bulb's filament
You return with lips of cinnamon in an amiable sentiment

I'm gracious towards this memory that we're making

It's all in your flavor that makes it all in my favor
We employ our tongues to work our passionate labor

Our wages are paid in interest to compound our love
My French accented heroine, your kiss might as well be my drug

I'm terribly and pitifully fixated to be addicted to it

The way you curl your tongue twirls my tongue dumb
Sensations pop my mind as if my tongue swirls in gum

We're floating within a bubble, encompassed by a passionate mysticism
You've proven that you're a repeat felon that falls victim to recidivism

You keep stealing and re-stealing my heart with your lips

Our lips have built a rapport, built a solid foundation
You steer my will, you are living trust that exudes patience

And like a wild mustang...

I race impulses of pleasure on your neurological highways
I advocate affection and action and I'm here in the present by way...

Of the Show me State

And as we further fuse together...

Your kiss becomes more and more full of TNT
You ignite my wicked tongue and the explosions run within me

You blow my mind

I feel the fullness of your lips rounding around mine
Our kissing action is powerful enough to induce sound from a mime

At least... an ooh or an ahhh

This kiss is a fantasy that we'll live until the 12th of never
It'll parallel the length of forty-four evers and be rated far better...

Than the best of the best of the best

As we kiss... we seem to make the whole room come alive

We rotate our mouths formation and spin circles in one spot
Your attraction grabs the attention of the whistling tea pot

The walls talk, conversing to one another of our fluent movements
The blinds voice their frustration since they can't see our movements

The chandelier resents the shine from our vibrant halos
As if we're Siamese twins joined at the hip, we'll always stay close

The living room's open curtains give view to the world
A perfected, connected instance of love between boy and girl

Anyone looking can see that a true connection does exist

The small table with your purse stands taller, it's proud
It's a part of a movie scene that could have only been written in the clouds

Passed out from being overwhelmed, the carpet is laid out over the floor
Science fiction stories can't believe us and yet the book shelves aren't bored

Our romantic scene is exciting and entertaining

The ceiling becomes our biggest fan as the leather chair sits in awe
Over looking our presence the fire wood keeps our movements logged

"These people must not be of this world"–F. Woods

We're the center of attention as we coalesce into one, from a pair
From the end of the hall way the first couple of steps stare

They're astonished

With our lips sweeping us throughout the galaxy like orbital debris
You're possessed with the spirituality of angels; it shows in how you kiss me...

Amen

Comets comment that we shine along side the sun's rays
Let's let the journey be the journalist to article on the front page...

Our kiss is breaking news

We've been written about in every daily, bugle, times, and press
We impress upon and brand into the minds of millions our simple caress

We're not at all overt in our demonstrations of affection
We're as subtle as wavy covers that sheet the sea's direction

We spill into one another even more

We'll keep crisscrossing tongues and hop scotching time
We've thrown our thrones across the regions of fantasy and combined...

The facts with the fiction

We've combined...

The means with the dreams

Combined...

The purpose with the mission

Combined...

The air with the wings

Combined...

The wants with the needs

Combined...

The truth with the lies

Combined...

The "thems" with the "we's"

And combined...

The fools with the wise

We've put together jigsaw puzzles of cultures and civilizations
We've painted the skies and aroused the greatest of visualizations

When mouths speak of beauty we're the figure of speech that's seen
We stand out and shine like golden beacons placed in all black scenes

How can you not notice our attraction?

Into the tree house of the fourth dimension, we climb winding ladders
We prolong the mixing of our imagination's imagery to form timeless batters

Because tonight... by all means... we will make love

Our tongues aviate our oral skies as our winged kisses were meant to fly
We add lipping to our mouth's ad-libbing though this arrangement wasn't
improvised

The universe had planned for this night to happen exactly as it is

Our pangs of love are appeased by the reliable relief of our kiss
We're the most esteemed relics since we've lived before history could even exist

*I believe that anybody who's anybody wants to experience a kiss like
this*

We've been sealed in a time capsule and whipped along galactic vessels
We've held kisses on every sun kissed shore until the tide has settled

And with poise...

We've rejoiced in tongues within the nucleus of prisms
Across the spectrum of light, Roy G. Biv tries to solve our riddle of prison

*Are we trapped in each others presence or are we free in each
others company?*

We're both

Even in this flesh world, you're my confidant and I'll forever stay confident
You help the pillars of my morals stand firm and add an extraordinary wealth to
my common sense

You've encouraged me to strive for life's hidden rivers

Encouraged me...

To understand that if I wanted to live then I had to be a life giver

You've encouraged me...

To un-mute my inner voice and to follow my destined path

Encouraged me...

To know that sharing halves the bad yet doubles the laugh

You are the fresh, invigorating air that has kept me alive
You are the distant horizon that I see just pass stormy skies

I shall forever strive to make you mine

You are the passionate paragon that sits in each of my mind's pockets
You are the praised and timeless piece of existence that rests on my chest like a locket

Seemingly...

We reverse time and grow younger and younger with each other
Today appears to be passing backwards and that makes us déjà vu lovers

Everything feels so familiar... we've done this before... and...

When our generous lips were ready and finally set to kiss
It was the physical equivalent to ears hearing beautiful dissertations of rhetoric

It's breathtaking and riveting

With candor, my exploring tongue meanders your mouth's maze
Wresting with your tongue, the surging adrenaline throws my body into a craze

I want more... I Want More... I WANT MORE!

I'm raging, my insides want you and my tongue wants all of you
I want to devour you by the hour until the reel of your desires is through

The impression I'm imprinting on your tongue is my explicit expression
I'm holding you, pressing myself on you while I'm continually stretching...

To reach into the depths of your mind

I feel your grasp on the sides of my stomach
Your touch increases the speed of the life that's in my blood running

While still involved in our French kiss...

You ease your roving hands from my midsection to my chest
You cautiously and slowly guide me to the wall to rest

You're so gentle with your force

My back presses against the taupe color Dutch boy paint
You pass out a spiritual lovingness to me as if your soul could faint

Know that I'll catch everything you could ever give

You grip the sides of my rib cage, you pull my shirt
You mix moans into whispering tones which makes my ears alert

I think to myself... why shouldn't I lie, cheat, steal, and kill?

Why shouldn't I lie awake all the time when my dream woman is here?

Or

Why shouldn't I kill time with her to make sure that she stays near?

Or

Why shouldn't I steal away any extra moment that I find to have a quick kiss?

Because ultimately...

I want to cheat death and slip into your ecstasy to ensure that I will always exist

Know this... I'll do anything for you

You restore my reasons for persisting through this life of mine
You tell me not to attempt but to just do, even though the times are trying

Delving in further retrospect...

We're physically living the future that we knew we'd always have
When we said that we'd still be together in 2009, the prophets all laughed

But... we're a self-fulfilled prophecy because we're still here... together

My French grip on your tongue, my gentle grip on your waist
Our grip on our fate and the strong hold from the grip of faith

They're all... unshakable

Even with our eyes closed I can see your peering jewels
Those diamonds sit in the jewelry box of my mind which will further fuse...

You into me... we into us... us into one

I feel that my mouth has been chosen for an intoxicating invasion
This investment is worth saving, I'm being abducted by a liaison...

Of Venus

You help me become acquainted with an exact patience
You're an enticing and hypnotic patient that prescribes me dosages of graces

You tell me... "Take one of these kisses a day and call me in your dreams"

Your delicate doctoring has undeniable dominion over my thoughts
Your wholeness is what my every desire has ever sought

I declare and I exclaim...

Your lip's touch could make psychosis seem like nothing strange
Though deranged, Schizophrenia sees what I'm saying to be normal and plain

Am I crazy? For you... yes!

It's been said that a picture is worth a thousand words
But a picture of our kiss would unable any combination of earthly words to accurately work

To try to sum up our eternal kiss with words... it would be...

Round about and endless circumlocution with rambunctious analogies
Constant comparisons with anomalies of divinely hippopatamic anatomies

And...

Distinctive definitions demystifying the fog of our unspoken dialogue
Concluded by a prolixity of complex sentences too enduring to have memories jog

They would tire... and to take an accurate picture of our kiss... To snap our spectacle...

Lenses would have to intensely focus
It would also need a panoramic unobservable feature to capture the invisible passion that soaks us

And...

This camera would need the most sophisticated amplification technology from E.T.'s
It would have to be able to look around the corner of tomorrow to finally see

That this kiss is... ahead of its time

We're the other's clues to an unsolvable case, a conduit for our intuit
We're the other's small yet persistent voice in the mind saying "always pursue it"

But... what is "it"?

"It" is...

The precise and exact recipe for a legacy

An...

Armory allowing only the forging of loving weaponry

"It" is...

The hypothesis of an exquisite chemist

The...

Subject of sentence, the allusions that have always hinted...

That this kiss of fire is a gift from the Messiah

"It" is...

The combination that unlocks a cherished vault

The...

Divine almanac of scores that we've always sought...

To beat

"It" is...

The prized contents of angelic archives

The...

Designing documents that constructs the solid foundation in our lives

We shall always aspire towards the attainment of "it"

I relapse, again swimming through the waves of my pondering
I remember we went up the hill to fetch water only to end up wandering

After we bumped our heads, we became crazier for each other
We made the world a playground as our tongues chased the other

All of nature was captivated by us

The winds howled with delight, the hills rolled with glee
Trees stood holding their trunks and not a leaf dared to leave

The nearby river rushed to get closer and to get the clearest view
Owls woke up to see the answer they've always wanted when they asked "Who?"

Who has discovered one of the requirements for eternal life?

The universe has unceasingly answered our love's prayer
We're sheeted with a tenderness that no force could tear

I'm deeply in love with you

For any second of the day, for any brief moment
When we aren't together my every body part screams from the torment

My hands...

Complain when they can't outline your fine face, luscious lips, or your awaiting waist

My eyes...

Cry, they say that without you in sight, their vision is a waste

My lips...

Confess their frustration when they aren't connected with yours

My brain...

Constantly drives and race thoughts around my mind with the pedal floored

My legs...

Tell me that they're tired and that they won't stand for this separation

My arms...

Can't muscle the strain, they want your hug within their embraces

The past scrap papers I used to describe my feelings for you are still smoking
Firemen know of the heat of my back drafts and why this living room is molten

We raise our hands to run along the others jaw line

As if guided by our latent intuition, we grab the others face and head
Since our fingers fondle hair follicles, we massage messages of the unsaid

We agree that...

From the sun's vibrant light to the night's mysterious dark
We'll strum on the strings of our hearts like a harp

And... we can never really be apart

We're intimately, intertwined within the neurons of the others spine
In first class seats of mental planes, jetting thoughts that pulses the others mind

Our connection is divine

I envision passing the celestial threshold into angelic ghettos
I'm in a platinum 3-piece suit; you glide on 24 karat gold stilettos

We breeze through the atmosphere being one with nature
Being one piece of moving art made by the creative Maker

I can hear your desires resonate from within your stare
I'm awed from your marvelous kiss; you make my soul so aware

Our vision is enhanced to the point where...

We can see the gravity of the situation, the magnetism of our attraction
The vapors of our passion, and this is the very reason that my spirit is everlasting

These types of moments last for eternity

We'll lay 69 to be intimately and infinitely melted as one
We're the hottest couple since the first pair of bubbles boiled on the sun

The dawn doesn't possess a brighter shine, one that could give sight to the blind
We'll let the past pass and here on Earth promise to never leave the other behind

We've become as happy as a child since we've reconnected with our other half

I realize that everything I seek in a woman you already have
Every quality you've ever dreamt a man to possess is what I already have

I also translate that...

I knew of you before memories could remember
You've been my greatest gift in every present before I ever knew of December

Your eyes are the reason that my pupils have learned so much
Your gentle hands are the reason that your speech leaves me touched

You're a governor of a passion that's state-of-the-art
Before Genesis could start, you were a prisoner of the chambers of my heart

Jailed to my every brain cell, you're mine, you are my mind
Your every inch of flesh is a second of eternity and I need more time

I need more time... to enjoy the more of you

As I reminisce your bliss, your kiss, my wish
You reappear in this, the energy expressed from my lisp

I love you

I am you, you are me, and we are us
We are everything that is honest, we lie in trust

We stare at each others thoughts using our mind's eye

You wink at me... I continue to tell you of my intentions

I want to love you in love with a lovingness that makes cupid blush
I want to love you until the winds hush and work tediously to sweep the dust of dusk

To be frozen in the molasses of your thick, icy hotness intrigues me
Let me be your gracious giver so that you can genuinely and wholly receive me

Take Me!!!

I want to love you in love until tears no longer fall from the pure eyes of doves
Until eternity no longer reaches and yearns for the comfort of a future hug

Until our bodies no longer carpet our magic rug

What's worse? To have never loved at all or to have loved and to have lost?

I'm not sure of the answer but I'll continue questing towards the question
I've learned that the joy is in the journey and the learning is in the lesson

So...

Learn of my desire to love you in love with a tender lovingness
Without you, watch me fall into the abysmal depths of nothingness

But... with you around... I notice that...

You add extra minutes to my hour and extra seconds to my minute
I'm a monumental apartment building and I want you to be my every tenant

You can pay rent when our timeless events that move us forward are spent
I love your sense and since you've camped out in my heart my mind is as open as pitched tents

Step in and make yourself comfortable

I enjoy making love to you without an erect penis
You encourage my ingenuity and I readily tap into direct genius

I want to fly kites of passionate words across your sensual sky
Raft on actions made of Braille and set sail on the infinite lake of your mind

Do you feel what I'm saying?

We can catch and capture our wishes like they're fishes
Make bon fires out of desires so we can roast and toast, my misses...

Your mister

Years and years ago I saw it...

I witnessed your elegant body in motion hinting towards your agility
I was lead to believe that being a hypnotist was just one of your abilities

The ways you expressed your divinity was in the upper infinity
You remedied my low energy by tenderly peeling grief to reach the depths of my inner me

And know that...

I'll crave for our touch until my bones have been reduced back to dust
Until the Irish run out of luck and until swans are seen as ugly ducks

How long would that take?

Your perfectly created shaped entity fits into me
Since creation, our binding bond was meant to be

As you still hold my head... you send messages to my mind... you say...

There's nothing that could stop us from being together
I'm going to stay your queen because I've been your queen forever

You're my prized king and in the flesh and I've come back to redeem you
You've been my dream too; you have a Velcro type of personality that I can't help but to cling to

Baby, you are the first and only man that I have loved unconditionally

Since I've learned how to speak, I've spoken your name
I've been awakened by your flame and become electrified during your reign

I've noticed that...

In these millions of years, you've changed yet remained the same
Though we've changed physical forms you've always cured my pain

I've seen you labor through the Southeastern Asian jungles
You fed me mangosteens and hushed my stomach's rumbles

You have always put my needs before your own

Right now on Earth, I give my word to always keep us together
If I ever think you're falling, I'd rip my wings off and give you their feathers

I won't let my angel hit the ground

You're my man, my friend, my thoughts, my concerns
My doctor, my collegiate professor from whom I'm ready to learn

I respond

I hear your speech and I'm falling deeper in love

You lead me on the path of Eternity, we can't lose track of time
We've grabbed the tail of comets and got blessed with an eternal shine

Our tongues further wrap around the other's like warm covers on cold bodies

You continue to tell me of you desires, truths, and wants
I'm easing into a tranquil state rarely achieved by Hindu monks

Your fingers input your thoughts directly in my brain... I hear you tell me...

My eyes were overjoyed to send your image to my brain
My brain was delighted to send the proper words for saying

I recall our first encounter as well

My sayings sailed through the atmosphere to land right in your ears
Your intelligence had made it obviously and evidently clear

My persona was in sync with yours

Our hearts connected simultaneously as did our souls
The windows of our spirit allowed the insight to see that our molecules were on cruise control

Our understanding was on one accord

Our soul's cover perspired and our heart beats sputtered
We quickly melted from ourselves and reality straight into the other

My mental ear detects more of your passionate words... you say...

You're like a blooming rose, so pleasing to my eyes
Magnificent like the brilliant stars that fill the night sky...

You are my sun

Your voice soothes my ears like the massaging songs of morning birds
To describe you, I don't think I could ever find the right words

Because...

You're more beautiful than gorgeous; you're more exotic than sexy
I ask what have I done for you to have found me and blessed me

That's something that I've always wondered to myself

You're more heavenly than an angel's harp melody
When I'm with you I feel that I am and will be forever free

You're my life; you're the dice I roll without chances
I can't lose; you're friendlier than Saint Francis

You've ignited me with the simplest and slightest glance
You made my heart sing joyously and my heart dance

You encourage my entity to be expressing and to never hold back
You're the general that leads my passion on missions of love filled attacks

You're the one man army that protects me from anything that could harm me

You are my king; you are the ruler of my galaxy
There's no place I'd rather be than right here with my love's battery

You charge me up

My mind floods with your emotion as we switch places
I put your back along the wall; I now translate my inner statements

Listen closely

I know words can't describe my love but I'll try to do it
I'll strap cords around my chest to the largest mountain and run until I move it

For you...

I'll catch falling stars, swim the seven seas and bring it to a kid who believes
Miracles happen and in my passing stay up late enough to tuck the Sandman to
sleep

I'll freeze the planet Mercury, melt Pluto and sleep with Venus to have a new birth
I'll actually shoot Venus with a shot from my penis to birth a new Earth

That's what I really mean

There will be nothing but love and to even get more real...
I'll surprise electric eels and leave them shocked since they knew the whales would have me killed

Nothing can deflate the ballooning love I have for you

I'll hop scotch across dozens of deadly fields of land mines
Fly outer space and repossess every UFO that's ever been flying

I'll patch the hole in the O-Zone layer with rolls of duct tape
Write poems in every language on every brick of the Great Wall of China for millions of months straight

I'll recite hot rhymes, stopping time until weeping willows stop crying
I'll never stop trying and that's my vow even after our knot's tying

Because...

You're like a roller coaster on cloud nine
A heavenly spectacle of glittering passion, you always shine

Our every encounter through our lives stays on rewind

You're an eternity of beauty trapped in a time space realm
We're brimming with possibility while we clutch attraction at its helm

Being above the clouds cannot stop our reign
You pour out intimate symbols that sit on the top of my brain

I've read your articles of clothing and comprehend that you're my current event
You'll always get every ounce of every bit of my energy that's spent

Your tongue smoothes over mine and I can't help but to moan
Sensations run throughout my body like they're a fine tooth comb

They search to find any inactivated nerve and...

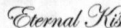

None are found since you've massage my every tendon
I know that to enter my every dream since the beginning was the universe's intention...

For you... and...

I'm glad that we're not kissing anywhere near Alaska
The heat from our lips would melt the snow and ice would cause a flooding disaster

But if we were... and did cause a flood...

I'd swim in your passionate pool, wade in your gentle grace
I'd twirl in your sensational swirl and drown in your welcoming waves

Only to be...

Reincarnated as a fish to eternally live within your ocean
I'd further breathe you and be completely covered by your devotion

Or maybe...

I'd come back as a rare tropical flower that only grows in your secret garden
I'd come back as a supernatural loofah pad to soften your soul if it hardened

Or maybe...

I'd come back as a sun ray, the one that could dry your tears
You'd mourn for me until you hear me as a melody that enters your ears

I'll be the sound of perseverance that you had to understand
Persisting pass problems presenting my persona as your perfect man

And as you already know... if I did die...

I'll resurrect revived, renewed, alive and true
I'm like the "T" and the "V"; I'll always stay around "U"

I choose to never abandon the pleasurable passion that you've handed
You're the finish line's tape that drapes over my fate, you've left me branded

With your kiss... you own me

You're so artistic in how you sketch my lips with your fine kiss
You're my palace's queen and I won't ever need to be reminded

You are my highness

You are absolutely my greatest of all inspirations
You're my exact reason that I'm so passionate and patient

I've always imagined us...

On a beach of pearls covered by white sands and stones
Actually, we'd be on a beach of pearls sitting on sand thrones

We're too far for anyone to mess with us, no one could mettle
I see brilliant trillion cut diamonds embedded in the most precious of metals

Platinum... sitting...

Wrapped around your tender little ring finger
We sit and listen to the Winds blow while the crashing waves act as back up
singers

I don't know exactly where this place is... but...

I know that it's only with you do I see this scene
This fantasy, our yet unlived reality, I'm kissing the figure for which I've always
dreamed

With your mind's eye acting as a scissor...

You cut and paste a colorful love on my mind
I intend to glue our bodies to the rhythm that will make our memories rhyme

We could make love out of our constructive vapors and construction paper
Hushed in the flavor of my favor, I'm elevating to the heights of sky scrapers

And...

As we ride the waves of pleasure, we seem to surf
We're transcending through the clouds and the stratosphere of Earth

I come to quickly find that...

There is no us without "u", you put the ease in please
It's just me and you flying and lying within our starry sea

What was once recognizable is now just a blur

From our view...

Earth is a swirl of whites, blues, greens and browns
Our kingdom is round; I'll make certain that my queen is crowned

And... your name... can't accurately describe you... and...

No amount on the highest price tag can measure your invaluable worth
Energy can't light more lamps than the way you light the world with the energy
your smile exerts

No poem could ever be more beautiful, sacred, or more endearing than you
Mathematicians say that it's irrational for us to be one, if it's me and you

But they just don't understand... love isn't always rational

Your kiss is the seed responsible for the growing love that's in my heart
Your lips are the shining bulbs on my the path to make sure I don't stumble in
the dark

You kiss me apart, and then you kiss me back together like I'm a puzzle
You comfort my struggle and my soul speaks to you when I thought it was
muzzled

With you...

I'm rich without wealth and I can fly without wings
We're a miracle and I know we can soar past anything

I don't want to be free

I want to be locked in your love; I don't want to find the key
Keep me here, I want to stay forever; I don't need to be freed

Open your rib cage to free your heart and you'll see me still sitting

I don't want to be independent of your kiss, it's becoming my habit
For this sensation I'll always be grabbing, I have to always have it

My heart beats in sync with your delectable gracefulness
I'm completely satisfied from your great kiss and graceful zest

I've left Destiny voicemails telling my desires and you've intercepted the call
You are my life line and I know that you will never, ever let me fall

You telepathically relate your mental vibrations

For certain, I will never let you free; you wouldn't ever want to leave
This kiss is only a small percentage to see and tonight you'll finally get all of me

I will be your every woman

Will Time eventually heal our wounds if tonight's scene of passion cuts?
I'll be beyond hurt if I can't ever again feel your gratifying touch

We'll keep directing and producing pleasure... all night long

Your kiss is the one serving of fortified syrup that I need to take everyday
Your lips are the abstract art pieces that I appreciate in its every way

Through our mental dialogue... you've somehow...

Slipped my mind into your mouth because you speak of my dreams
Your mind's whispers ring loudly and I know exactly what you mean

You remove your own inhibitions as our kisses flow like a stream
There's not a fault that could make me not see you as pristine

Mistakes can't blemish your image to me... my love sees pass that

You're of the likes of the most high and rare heavenly beings
You've slipped my mind into your mouth, now you speak of our dreams

You are finesse

You add the grace to every place; seduction is the make up of your face
You add the eloquence to life's every sequence and you started the human race

Everyone who knows you exist, frantically hope to run into you

Like them, I need you... and I need you...

Like the early bird needs the worm

I need you...

Like my flame needs our match to make our kiss burn

I need you...

Like how wings need the air for flight

I need you...

To not end the events of tonight

Piloting our mental planes, we soar around the cosmos
We're esteemed and aspiring to be the next idols of astrological models

This kiss is like...

The sun to the sky or the water to fish
The butter to pancakes, the genie that grants our wish

It's the perfect match for my lips... it's above comparison

I've written my secrets for a woman like you everyday
I etched them in the sands of distant shores praying that they'll always stay

And stand through the waves of separation

Every night...

I've wished for your character to be written into my life
It's like you were poured from the big dipper and the next day your shine dripped
into my eyes

You're more than a trophy; you're a natural prize with no game show
In every way imaginable, you're more, you're a gold treasure with a smile as
beautiful as rainbows

The kiss that we're sharing right now is atomic
It was never written for our relationship to ever remain platonic

Truly...

Your kiss to me is more valuable than the U.S. Treasury's mint
You're my tender lender that's been loaned to my sixth sense

So...

I'll do my best to be the best out of all the rest, out of all the tests
I'll give all of all my flesh and I promise that we'll be together even after there's
nothing left

We embrace each other tighter

We're coiling ourselves together tighter than the springs in a small watch
We're basking in the sensations of pleasure, being two lovers on this floating rock

Everything about you exudes shine like glistening jewels
You move and groove in and out of my mental visual views

I want you to...

Steer me, navigate grace to spread throughout this place
Consume and digest me into the tune that you will always play

Before you came back to rejoin my soul...

My life was lived in the dark but this kiss has sparked our spark
You've pulled on my inner chords and your light has lit our start

We have a bright future ahead of us... and...

As we converse in fluent French at a passionate and steady pace
We seem to alleviate the force of gravity and lovingly levitate

Our mouths speak the volumes of our concealed feelings
We're elevating chills and holistic remedies of healing up to Heaven's ceiling

We'll leave this flesh behind because we shall remain eternal
Inscribe your vibe between my soul's sheets; let me be your journal

Write me right!

This kiss arches, whips, flips, and swirls around my thoughts like calligraphy
Your mouth is so inviting, all my spirit keeps yelling is "Come live with me"

Come live with me!!!

You write eclectic passages on my mind with your lips
I jaunt along the trail you blaze on my brain through its turns and dips

It's amazing...

Tingling chills repel up and down our backs using our spinal cords
The aura of our essence flees through our skin escaping through our pores

Your kiss is...

Sweetly soft

You are...

My idea of woman

Your kiss...

Can't be bought

You are...

My ideal woman

You are charming, beautifully alarming, you're without equal
The purest of all people, in my mind's heart is where I'll securely keep you

We're making love without sex or elaborate chemistry kits
With the touch of every finger that creeps, we enter into a deepening bliss

And... like a soup of love...

We're warming each other up with a simmering heat
We translate affirming affection while letting our entities speak

You engrave the signature of your lips on the awaiting walls of my heart
My mental canvas is also colored with your superior strokes of art

Before you came back to me...

My cup of life had runneth over with emptiness, but we're back intimate
We're resuming our grooving, traveling through the winds of sins growing more innocent

We're being purged the further our tongues surge

This kiss is getting more and more passionate, growing fiery
You know all of my desires and yearnings because you are the pages of my diary

You provide the flesh for my fantasy

Even as classmates in the University you were considered a star student
You didn't laugh when you taught me what a muse meant, you still possess that prudence

I questioned you... "Are you the offspring of Summer?"

You said that you were, and also of many other things

I questioned you... "If you came from Earth, do you know you'd be its 8th world wonder?"

You said that you did, but that you weren't concerned with titles from human beings

You only concerned yourself with me and my thoughts

From that day we've spoken French and Italian on a thousand islands
We've conceived diamonds and discussed designing with ancient Mayans

"That pyramid is perfect... you don't have to change anything"

Every time I think of your kiss, wherever and whatever I have that hurts heals
This mystical kiss is mythical; it's an urban legend that cannot possibly be killed

It will survive...

Within the pictures of a mute society

Survive...

Within the hymns of vibrating gems

Survive...

Within the prayers that are requested silently

Survive...

Within the hearts of her and him, and them

Not only my mouth, but also my being is saturated with your kiss

The language of our body is explicitly simple, aggressive yet gentle
Our heat could entice frozen flames to once again rekindle

We'll say... "Your love can burn again... just continue to believe and work hard"

As I grip your spine you still hold a grip on my mind
My memories want you back and the best present is this current time

Being each others better half...

We give each other our undivided attention
Our souls listen as our mind's eyes twinkle and glisten

Even our minds can't take their eyes off of each other

We're two lovers, together forever in one love
Combining passionate pureness, our sum could equal a million and one doves

We're two instruments that play a silent song of love in perfect key
We recite lyric-less poems as our tongues gleefully run free

Our entities intertwine sensibly and tenderly
Our conference of a loving homage echoes throughout the world within a breeze

Within each gust of the wind

We're only concerned with keeping our lamp of adoration burning and lit
We embrace each other as equals; we don't really need to wish

Yes...

We have done things that could be the wish of millions
We've had wings and have been able to fly since we were children

Remember the first time we went on a date?

We flew through the sky and ate lunch on the tops of clouds
The O-Zone's layer of seats sat the angels of our divine crowd

They love to see actions of pure love

We orchestrated thunderstorms into a symphony of pleasant tunes
We've dampened worlds with our reign and this is truth...

In any form of anything... I'd be able to please you

If I were an SUV...

You wouldn't have to worry about my suspension
You could get lost with my features and use GPS to find my intentions

You could drive me and park me in loving space like you're Cupid's valet
I'd comfort your back with my leather and I'd never break down on tough terrain

You'd be the only one who had the keys to turn me on
My stereo's acoustic passion would easily put you in the zone

If I could be the water in the ocean...

I wouldn't ever in any way, shape or form wave goodbye
From under your toes to over your head, my touch would close your eyes

You could float

I would have your back and I would always support you
My number one mission is love and I'd never abort you

And it's destined that...

This king and queen will one day birth a prince and princess
I love you because you activate all of my senses

Sight, smell, hear, taste and touch

Throughout these thoughts you've invited me into your world
Your mouth is so hospitable in the welcoming of your unpredictable twirl

Hello, once again

You are the one lady I'll share with all that I have to give
For just a blown kiss from your lips a million dollars would be my opening bid

With such a fond touch and a warm kiss...

You've given me a new light on a new life, a new flame for an old name
New thoughts for what I've sought and you've balanced out my brain

Your kiss is like spiritual candy, you've filled my soul's cavity
I'm multiplying reasons to return affection to you at bunny rabbit speed

You're so calm yet ferocious in with your kindness
This moment we're sharing tonight is unending, it's timeless

I reckon... you are the finest

You're the kind of one that's one of a kind
The kind one that makes our every event one for the times

You make normal events classic memories of love

It's never been about any one thing that has attracted me to you
We have agreed on a singular reason that has made us true

Our realization... love is love all the time

We're moving in the same direction with ordained affection
We said that before we could be that we had to share our confessions

And so... we did...

I remember your emotion spilling, I recall my feelings
We've dealt with the dealings and we've cured the illing...

Since we've cleansed the other...

Our souls dance together to the rhythm of our existence
Our hearts do our souls listening; our tongues show urgency and persistence

We douse the other with kisses that coat the other's body with hope
We've dug to the surface of the land to dissipate within atmospheric smoke

We've blazed from the earth's core to sweep as the wind

We've touched every skin and every hue-man
We've been the countless tunes that have always grooved man

We've been caught in some troubling plights though

You've rode in giant pumpkins and lost slippers
You've fallen into a sleep that could only be awakened from my kisser

I've been in a tumbling plight, in which I thought I'd never, never land
You've been the beauty that saw that beyond the snare of a beast was a man

People may say we're a fairy tale but we know we're real

You cast future occurrences of us in my distant thoughts
The mirages aren't mirages because when I move closer they aren't lost

I know what they are... they're...

Reflections from the future looking back at this moment in the past
Presents open the door into the moment of today, now will eternally last

I clutch you closer, we're chest to chest

I serenade you with cascades that are made from a pure love
We promenade within the blanket of passion as our lips hug...

Like once forgotten but now reunited lovers

You have the sweetest kiss, the softest tongue
From the purest part of perfection your mouth has been swung

You have the smoothest skin, the most precise touch
I'm stuck; an overdose of your potent kiss is just enough

And I admit... I can handle it

My taste buds are craving for more of your flavor, more of your uniqueness
Blindfolded in a dark room, a cross-eyed blind man could clearly see this

My breath is becoming yours... my body is becoming yours

I hear how your desires sing of future pleasures
I'm sinking into you chest to release your latent treasures

I spread this kiss over your mind until it's smothered
Let this passionate gravy over flow in your mind's eye, lose sight for all others

I'm the one you have your eyes set on

For the joy of loving you, what can I say?
Let me inscribe into your heart the elation I feel for you every hour of every day

You groove and sway into my vibration's rhythm making my belly dance
Intuition jumps from my gut in channels of chakra that cultivate romance

We focus

We've ruled continents; we've had statues made of our grace
There are winds of fire that swirl within our kiss strong enough to make the earth
quake

I put my hand on the wall as I bump you backwards
The slight stumble to the wall didn't shake up the swerve of what we serve

Love's dish will still be digested tonight

While holding the wall I hear some of the conversation it's having
It's excitedly babbling and I can make out a couple of sentences between all of the
laughing

Her hair smells so good; if I had hands I would grab it without thinking

Ha, haa, hee, hee

Look at the pictures over there staring, will they ever start blinking?

Ha, haa, haah

I dismiss this instantaneous insight

It's like your tongue has fangs and your kiss bites into my brain
The sensations tap my main veins and surges my main frame

I'm freezing hot

We conduct a symphony of energy and we're intimately intentional
We're covering each other with an ardent armor, our love is invincible

My craving for you is limitless, it's insatiable
You can't be edited, you're irreplaceable, and that's why my soul has always been placed in you

You're the one that I've loved first, you're my first love
You have a spout on your chest to pour your heart out to me when I thirst love

I will drink your holy water

My tender heart knows that you're the one to mate with my soul
It also knows that I'm the vehicle but you're the tires needed to roll

In a gist...

I can say that it's not paralysis
My body is only stiff from the exquisiteness of your kiss

And yet... I still move toward your gift

We're leaning into each others day dreams like we're italicized
We're open minded, there aren't any ways for our talents to hide

Or... our thoughts of each other

Your kiss locks within my chest as a keepsake, I'm kept safe from danger
Speaking of you being jailed to my brain cells and my heart chambers...

Doesn't that make you my... in-mate?

And I also knew from that first day I saw you...

I didn't really want to smell you; I knew what that would lead to
As if I was wearing lead shoes I knew that it would be hard for me to leave you

Beating each other a better path, we give direction to our senses
The silent air listens as our spirits converse in passionately compound sentences

You are my soul mate and I've always had you within me

Your wettest muscle swims in the stream of my consciousness
You sideline my fear, settle my ego and diminish my pompousness

You've been my favorite color in its every tint and shade
You've been the hint and way, the words spoken in print and phrase

I reflect my opinion when I send vibrations to you about this kiss
We're kissing champions whose lips could fill the grandest of canyons with bliss

Your images in my mind make my hearts contents content
The low melody of love that plays in my thoughts is one that I can hum with

Hmmm, I do love her, hmm, hmmm, hmmmmmm... yes I do

I'm emptying my heart and soul into the feelings of this kiss
Each layer of your lips warms me, the heat steadily persists

And... as if you have majored in geography...

You've studied the layout of the land between "we"
You're a natural physicist and you understand the importance of inertia and speed

We'll keep our motion and velocity until an outside force acts upon us

It's more about what you don't say that I understand
It's more about my invisible cape that makes me your wonder man

Come more into me, I want you closer...

Closer than the many of the most
Closer than the water with the bottom of boats

So that we can...

Feast in the delicious heat of you and me
The us and we, the pieces of speech and the how we celebrate tomorrow's eve

From now until forever never comes...

Tear ducts won't be used much and our attraction won't rust
I don't plan to lose your touch even if my hands couldn't feel your clutch

My memories could never forget

Pieces of our wishes are carried with each word that we kiss
Pieces of our soul are translated with every glance we give and get

We have hearts full of passion, veins that house flames
We have brains focused on fame with thoughts that have always trained...

To keep us in shape... perfect shape that is

We have muscles of hustle that have strengthened through the struggle
We share a pair of hands that can divide evil into even lesser troubles

I've camped out in your open mind, set fire to your hurt
I've arranged the proper plot of our story and put disappointment in the dirt

It's been destiny that has seen what's left in me
She told me that I'm blessed to breathe and to readily accept the fee

I had to endure 26 years on this Earth without you... that was my price

Our souls can't grow old while our right words are unlocking special codes
We've been dressed to show, we're fashioned head to toe in Hope's robe

The threshold of romance bowed and the cove of our soul glows
We have rolled and strolled the road of gold with our emotions exposed

In the past when we flew under Love's weather

We sought therapy terribly even though the ailing didn't hurt
We became physicians, delving into the practices of healing that have always worked

Those practices are of pure love

We know that with great power comes great responsibility
Our inner divinity blending with our angelic chemistry creates our celestial affinity

Let tonight be an illustration of greatness

Let's leave a doctrine for all the ones who can't watch
Our particular combination is safe and our legacy's recipe is Cajun hot

You weigh on my consciousness...

You can lie on me; put the pressure over my every limb
Grind my mind with joyous times, you are my sacred gem

We fit within one another without puzzle pieces boxing us in
I'll answer when your body cries out to me and if you ever again drop your chin...

Though I don't imagine you doing so...

I'll bend to my knee to plead with your soulful sea
I'd console in thee, opening my heart and hand exposing the golden ring

Will you marry... you know you're my Venus right?... and... so will you...

I'll stay the mirror that reflects your magnificent passion
The beautiful brown skin that caresses your body and that which you'd be wrapped in

Because I...

I can be whatever you need me to be but I can't be without you
No skeptic can doubt you and whispers dare each other to shout to you

Shhhh... I dare you to scream her name

I'll handle you with care and my respect won't allow me to stare
Though each feeling of this kiss leaves me steadily entranced, I don't care

Because...

I want you more than paintings can show, more than stars can glow
You deserve all the credit, without you, there simply isn't a show

All my life, I thought it was about...

About my love, my passion, my drive, my desire
My heart, my mind, and my insides that are filled with fire

But you've shown me that...

It's about our intentions, our dimensions, and the limits fences...
That we erupt through without any pause or any flinching

It's about our family and the words of our granny
It's about your gratitude towards my actions that make me feel manly

Our mistakes, our missed takes that we should've taken
It's about our perseverance that keeps us moving though we're shaking

It's about our friends who encourage our right doings
To our curiosity that keeps us when, where, how, why, and whoing

You've also shown me that...

It's still about me and that I have to keep my mind mine
Not to allow intervention from negativity though it's been desperately trying

You eliminate hate's lure and cure the eyes that see illusions and rage
It's about my belief that reminds me that I am saved

All things I want to make are have already made... with you and I together...

It's about our imagination; it's so vibrant and so vivid
It's about our wildest dream, demanding that we live it

My life, has been about me, it's been for you
It's about realizing my own goals and remaining true

My life, has been about us, it's about what we do
It's about realizing our goals and forever remaining true

We're inebriated from the intoxicating basis of our loving greatness
Dizzying in the cyclones of our tongues this kiss kind of makes us...

To a certain degree... storm chasers

Your lips are expensive and valuable, exclusive and precious
The direct opposite of expiring, this eternal sensation intends to mesh us...

Into inseparable pieces of fabulous fabric

Your lips seep between the spaces of my skin, kissing my melanin
The glow encompassing our bodies is intensifying, it's yellowing...

Becoming more brilliantly golden

Your kiss is like...

The mist over the lake at dawn

My kiss is like...

The art, the magnetic paint that keeps you drawn

Your kiss is like...

A loving pillar that keeps me standing

My kiss is like...

A runway, eagerly awaiting more and more of your lips landings

Your kiss is like...

A pure connection, attraction, love, and passion

Our kiss is like...

The perfect now, before, and the future event that will always happen

And I don't have to question...

If I gave you my life, would you kill time with it
If my love was the answer to enigmatic rhetorical questions, would you still get it

If I gave you the mirrors of my intentions would you reflect them back to me
If my train of thought raced to please you, would you get on the right track with
me

If we did yoga together could we stretch tonight into two nights
If my tongue traced your long legs to the base of your triangle, would it be alright

Because I know you will and that it would be fine

Well let me answer some of the questions you may have
Yes, I will love you when you cry and sigh, no, we won't always laugh...

At least on Earth

If you bark and hiss, yes, the problem will be fixed
No, I'm not a do-it-yourselfer, so I'll need your help for our interdependence

All night long, if you're asking me how long will I listen to you
Passionately, is my answer when asked how will I stay kissing you

No, is my resounding exclaim if asked can I live without you
Life without you, I'll answer that my world would be a vibrant, radiant rainbow of
no hue

Your "I love you" echoes and floats down the middle canals of my ears
Cutting through the confusing fog like glass shears your kiss keeps the meaning
clear

I've come to see...

You weren't too far; my dream was not too far fetched
I've been kissed by Venus and now you've left me star pecked

You are my everything

You're the ray to this son, the completed product when I'm done
The reasons we've come together is because the inner course stimulated our
spinal rungs

You reverberate my vertebrae with a genuine interest
You're my battle; "us" will be won even if I have to lie in trenches

I will fight for this

I'll sacrifice my life twice and fall from the highest realm
To oversee your dreams of fantasies until your awakening leaves me overwhelmed

For forever...

Yes, I am here, hearing what your soul expects
Yes I'm here, to give you all of me, and I know you accept

I want to revel in the randomness of our conversation
I want to freely glide through the elation of waiting

The best things come to those with patience... that's why I'm patient

I've never lusted over your passion or over your physique
I admire the pitch of your voice, the substance of your speech

I admire....

The glance of your eyes, the slant of your brows
I don't consider today a present if you aren't beside me now

I want to fondle your muse, solve our clues
Poeticize your jewels through poems that help to widen the world's view...

To see that a love like this exists within every person alive

Everything that we discuss makes us introspective detectives
We choose to delve into the others soul like we're taking spiritual electives

We receive "A's" for being Angelic

I want to revel in the randomness of your ocean
Your kiss shocks and flows through me like electronic rivers; this kiss has
e-motion

Let me drift into your every mental crevice, your every thought
Let me be the North Star to your desires, with me you will never be lost

You connect with me; we frequently walk across a golden gated bridge
My chest has a tattoo that says 'hers' and yours says 'his'

The next million nights that we share will be grand
We'll fly and soar each other's loving sky and couldn't even if we wanted to land

*You see... we were never too comfortable with walking... so we've
always flown*

From my side to yours, I want your side with mine
I want to side with your mind, I want to further seduce the seconds of time

So that they can pause... because...

I want them to pause just like I did when I saw your face
Just like my heart did when I felt your grace and when my lips met your taste

I am your rose, cemented into your favorite garden
Tonight, when it comes time to consummate the mission, I'll be your passionate sergeant

I'll command my fingers to search, my kiss to secure the parameter
Command my private to break down walls and my tongue to salvage the damages

You'll be my prisoner of war... tonight you'll scream from pleasure when we... POW!!!

My ears have cried for your sound, my eyes have heard your language
My thoughts of explicit situations have always been deliberate, always been flagrant

Your kiss writes musical notes on my brain, grooving my memory
Your kiss sings songs with sting, its passion buzzes around tenderly

Honey, tonight your kiss...

Wraps around my head like a bandana
Your lips peel away my love scars like a banana

You sing this song like it will be your last
Let's let time freeze for a night and act like our song will never pass

Since our lips have made contact, I've been high

You make me see things that were blocked by my own rage
Blocked by my own pride and my own self judgment, you're the key that frees me from an unlocked cage

You've been beautiful in your every shape and in your every shade
You're the most desired fad that in no way or form could every fade

It has been you that has made me
You, you're the reason that God lets man breathe

You... are love

You've gotten closer to me by coasting me over the distance
You've stirred my emotions with no hands, you're so persistent

And my kiss...

Must remind you of an evening's breeze
Being that it's so gentle in touch yet yielding much power to please

I feel you relaxing; seemingly into a waking trance... you're getting sleepy

My kiss further slides into my mind like butter in a hot skillet
The sight of the pictures in your minds eye touches your soul and soothes you when you feel it

You grip my arms tighter

My weather worn heart was beaten; I'm now your precious antique
This is revitalizing me into a new and improved soul mate, so to speak

Of our kiss and our love...

Circumstances won't change it

Of our kiss and our love...

"Unconditional" defines it

Of our kiss and our love...

Situation can not sway it

Of our kiss and our love...

The world will always be reminded

From the eyes to my mind and from thoughts to my tongue
You're everywhere I am and every prize that I've won...

Magnified by a zillion

Your stamina for kissing is...

Inexhaustible

My stamina for love is...

Infinite

Our stamina for changing the world's view of love is...

Influential

From the serious possibilities of me and you
To the soft utter of the words "I do"

My passion for you only increases

From sports coliseums and museums and monuments
From 6 star hotels and restaurants to no condom hints

My passion For You only increases

From the time your knock hit the door
To the moment our clothes line the floor

My passion For You only Increases

From that first day of our first child
To the day we attract the funeral's crowd

My Passion For You Only Increases!!!!

From the shining stars to being seen as shining stars
Let's toast to our future, the world is ours

The world is ours... it is ours

On a planet without gravity I would have still fallen for you
If somehow I was born without a voice I would have still been calling for you

Saying... "I will find you... I'm on my way"

You've given me a feather in which I write my rhymes
It's as angelic as you are and it makes me feel divine

Just like your name... so tonight... lie for me

Allow me to paint passionate coats of color over you
We'll co-create a vivid country of fantasies that we can rover through

Let me unlock your hair and swim within your mind
I'll ring your cerebellum with a tender grace that'll travel down your spine

Lie for me...

Let me savor the chocolateness of your kiss
Our every tryst has been accompanied with an absolute bliss, you are my granted
wish

You're the piece that completes me, my puzzling life is whole
You're the spirit of my soul; you and I were cast out of the same mold

How incredible is that?

I've slept soundly knowing that I was safe in your keeping
You've been the natural harvest that I've been reaping and the springs of Heaven
have been leaking...

Because...

Everyday you drip onto me a liquid as rich as the tea from celestial kettles
Your chest is the destined land of my love and within your heart I pleasingly settle

*This is familiar ground... I've been here in my dreams plenty of
times*

Our tongues swirl and twirl in our kiss like calligraphy symbols
You're the most desired view of man's eye and you've been outside of my soul's
windows

*You can't be taken out of my sight... physically or mentally... or
spiritually*

A heart is a home and in my heart, this is where you reside
Tonight, lie for me, next to me, forever, stay by my side

Until my strength leaves my body...

I'll push you up and make sure you know that I'm always here
I'll always hear, your every slight whisper for appreciation will be reflected my
dear

Lean on me, let me be your pillar of courage
Let me be your passionate translator of affection when your speechless mouth
can't word it

If you had some type of vibrational x-ray you'd see that...

My soul has your hand print, you've touched the inner me
My spirit is entwined with your essence and I'll always remember she

You, her and...

Every form of woman that you've been in my life
You're my dream site, the queen type, and that's clear to see like pristine ice

Since...

I've worn platinum suits and swept my angel right off of her golden stilettos
The crowd whistled like tea kettles as they deemed our dance special

Though my time is limited tonight... here's what I'd like to do

I'd like to swim into your mind, make your every hurt feel fine
Outline your design with these hands of mine until like a star you shine

Glimmering and shimmering forever

I'd like to massage your visage with kisses that seem odd
I'd take your moans and ahh's to paint and arrange them into a collage

Your impression on my heart is pure impressionism

You don't understand how I want your image to stay imprisoned in my brain cells
You make my frame sail; I don't think you understand that Cupid aims well

Only with intentions can a person miss love... but we won't

Your body was built for Cupid's arrow dynamics, for me to manage
To not be taken for granted and for this son to always tan it

Soak in my loving rays of adoration

My passion is blazing; you've been the imagery of poetic phrasing
You impregnate me with patience, you are so, so amazing

Know that my love for you sometimes turns me into an animal

I'd like to be thrown into your rib cage to live in love
Your heart would be my prison; I'll take my time for exactly what it was...

Rehabilitation... and question how can I work out a stronger love?

Of all of you, I'd like to be intertwined, entangled, and entrenched
Your kiss is why I exist and never from your high class could I be dismissed

I'll be here until I'm summa cum laude of Eternity's graduating class

We're together, tough as leather able to weather any weather
Whether it made us swelter of where we sought the heat of wool knit sweaters

Soul mate, know that you're wanted and needed...

Leprechauns want your kisses back in pots
Romance authors want you back in plots

You are needed

Fairy tales need your message to continue the dreaming
Winds need your flowing scent to keep on streaming

You are desired... not just by me but by everyone

I'd like to build a palace of kisses with your lip prints on ever brick
It would be as big as big could get, through the clouds it would stick

It's...

Your entity's energy

Your...

Angelic divinity

Your...

Definitive amenities

Our...

Affinity that'll last for infinity

I'll remedy every sore joint with massages that message love tenderly
It's now my time to be your all, to finally be the man I was always meant to be...

Your rightful King

We were chosen and woven within an intangible knowing
We're radio active and glowing; we're the direct opposite of slowing

We're gaining momentum

This type of kiss couldn't be held to the exclusivity of one ethnicity
Our passion has permeated all the hues of flesh throughout history

Repeatedly... you've been every woman... I've been every man

My number one goal has been to capture the soul that has possessed your kiss
Your mouth is the "X" of my trip, my goal that I vowed to fully commit

I'm losing myself in this kiss

I'm leaving myself with you, I overlook us from out of my body
I see the vibration of energy surrounding us within this living room of a lobby

I see your spirit leaving your fleshy cast; you join me above the action
You whisper to me about your elation, my passion and of our attraction...

"Isn't it perfect?"... I reply "Absolutely"

You don't necessarily have a coke bottle shape body but you got that pep, see
You unlock and let me, you sincerely respect me and freely you direct me

I'm enjoying the sights of this out of body experience

We swirl around the room like ghosts in the fashion of incense smoke
We've always held on to the faith and expectance for this type of passionate hope

Look at how we kiss, look at our we move
Look at how you hold, isn't our fluidity smooth?

Tonight...

Has been made a new day and we've found paths for a new way
We've seen new stars shimmer in a new space; our mirrors will reflect a new face

Right now...

I'm feeling old habits becoming new waste and I'm taking the trash out today
I'll model the motto of a new phrase; our wars have a new wage

Yes we can

We're finding our way through a new maze, letting our eyes stare a new gaze
Our stage is set for a new play on love serious enough to introduce a new age...

Of dramatized, theatrical performances

You've laid your head on my chest like an honorary medal
Of your soft, angelic hands, know that I'll never let go, I'll never let go...

I'll never let go... I'll always remember...

We've eaten lunch on cloud nine and listened to the blues on the moon
I placed one of Saturn's rings on your finger and I became a galactic groom

We dipped in the Milky Way and rained chocolate kisses to Hershey
You got pregnant by the son of the sun and then you birthed seas

Our ecstasy poured into the universe

You cover the world with oceans as deep as our devotion
I excitedly spun around in the middle of the cosmos and the planets still haven't
stopped their circular motion

Like the planets, my head still spins when I realize that you're mine...

I see Heaven every time I stare into the depths of your soul
You're in another league with how you hold and share your control

I swim within the lake of your pondering, I am your thoughts
You're everything I've sought and there isn't enough time to be bought

You're a timeless blessing...

You'll outlast the minutes, hours, days, months, and years
You've surpass the levels of fear and for eternity you've been here

And you'll stay here... with me... and I with you

You are of the truest and purest divine design
You bungee jumped into my nervous system using the cord of my spine

Your kiss has an extremely calming effect on me

This craft of technique can only be seen with a minds eye
I'm along with the days in a daze of dreams when I rest beside your side

Thank you... I love you for loving me

Of my dreams and the starring woman in my fantasies
You give direction to my ramblings and I know that we'll start a family

How you got dealt in the past without me is why I'm your king of hearts
How I got dealt in the past without you is why you're my queen of hearts

Though we seldom admit it...

We both had been in and liked the comfort of the dark
We both brought to the other that streaming and loving spark

We'll stay on a new level with our passionate expressions
You poetically put kisses in rhyme; your unspoken words are full of affection

Whenever I want to leave earth, I hear a poem of yours
You flow Heavenly, like a church choir singing with angels playing the right chords

Your flow makes me think and really appreciate good reciting
It's good and exciting; you take me on pleasurable, psychological hiking

Tonight, you've taken me around the world...

I've been swung over the seas

I've been...

Bounced throughout eras

I've been...

Swept within the breeze

We've been...

Released from life's terror

I'm clamping to your heart with a bear trap type kiss
Your spirit wears my lip marks with pride; I'm the most vicious lover that has come to exist

My kiss reaches out for you though it lacks actual arms
My lips amaze you and lace your pucker with a factual charm

Since I've met you...

In my heart and on my mind is where I've kept you
You've always been right with me, there's no way that I would have left you...

Anywhere that I'm not

Your kiss is sweeter than the grandest of charmers
You continuously dig in my thoughts like farmers and Tranquility calls on you to have you calm him

You're majestic

We're a mystery that need not be solved
Our story's problem couldn't be wrong and in connection with you, the seconds crawl

We've lived...

Under the water, on the land, and in the air

We've lived...

As dragons lunging long tales of love from dungeons and lairs

We've lived...

In the heart, in the art

We've lived...

In the life of lives, being alive with life

We've lived...

In the soul of the speech, within the stomp of the march

We've lived...

As separate units of oneness yet remained husband and wife

We've lived in the heat of the sun in a binary world being the only ones

Later on tonight...

We'll become wrestlers, making the bed our ring
You'll become my wife, once I present that ring

Our love is stronger than garlic cloves and vinegar shots
I know that I'm the winner she got and even in December she's hot

Yes you are... and all of a sudden...

The visions of tonight are rushing back to me, passing in a blur
Asia, Africa, Rome, Heaven, Russia, your blue skirt

All of the places and things we've done... the...

Ancient languages of love, symbols, signs, the speeches
Infinity, celestial monoliths, rivers of time, how our future reaches...

Around the curve of tomorrow

I see our tongues jumping, twirling, romancing and dancing
I see us in the Camelot prancing and in the hallways of Fantasy's mansion

I see us...

Eating breakfast on the moon and singing old songs
Laying under huge palms, your hand in my palm as we read proverbs and psalms

Who can find a virtuous woman? For her price is far above rubies

I see myself with eight legs and us kissing as the sun's heat fled
I feel the heat of Ecuador and hear of all the desires that weren't said

If I never get another memory then let me speak a piece

Take my hand and follow me while I lead you
You're an imperative part of my life, I need you

So... let me lead you

I don't want you screaming my name or moaning
I just want you to be here, stay with me a million mornings

I want to dance with you on beach Bliss
There is not a millimeter of your entertaining flesh that I'd leave un-kissed

Tonight...

We kiss each others lips with a touch that's softer than the bottoms of baby cotton balls
We have re-awakened the living rooms of distant dreams causing all the eyes of time to pause

Bearing witness to a testament of miracles... all of my Earthly life...

I've wanted to rotisserie your urges; spin you into a cocoon of pleasure
Amor-all your heart and smile so they'd be able to withstand the harshness of any weather

I've wanted to pull the splinters from your feet and knees
Wanted to put muscle rub on your back, I know it's been uncomfortable praying for me

Let me soothe you... completely... tonight and for all the rest of tomorrows...

Follow me; please listen to my actions and not just my words
I'll travel the world over and under to bring you a billion ways to say those three
words

I'll translate every dialect... human and animal

I'd rent an igloo and bet the owner that my love for you could melt it
The strongest sensations, I've felt them, the most delectable scent, I've smelt it

Please...

Make memories with me until we forget that we're not two different people
Dissect my body; open my soul to split my spirit and people will see where I keep
you

Even if I become victim of insomnia... I'll dream about your eyes

They sparkle like melting ice yet hold the warmth of a hundred furnaces
The most rewarding prizes require the hardest work and I've enjoyed earning
this...

Kiss... so...

Take my hand, let me lead you, follow me
We'll surmount all events because I've never seen problems, I've only seen
opportunities

*You place your hands to my jaws and send me your forget me nots...
through brain waves you say... Tonight...*

We'll be so intertwined that you won't be able to tell your parts from mine
Your kiss is the bomb like mines and intoxicatingly tasting like wine

Know that...

I'll be your children's mom, your wife; I'm your soul mate and lover
No other could arouse you enough for you to allow them into our covers

I leave no room for error... you continue

I wear a crown because you've given me a royal love that's only fit for a queen
I assure you that your visions haven't been dreams and death has never been able
to end our means

I love you

In the mid-night our bare bodies will hibernate in our natural state of affairs
We'll let nature's oil lubricate us; you'll sip from my fountain of youth with
delicate care

You don't have to share... my juice is all yours

You smile and continue I also...

See the galaxies that we've passed as we sailed on comets
I feel the colorful breeze from the times we've kissed in kaleidoscopic tropics

You have taken me to heavenly paradises

I remember and can see my tear stains in San Francisco
I also see how we've danced; each star glittered like the center piece in a disco

We've been having a ball together for a long time

You have a nice voice, you possess a brilliant mind
You are physical poetry living in rhymes, you're a rare find

You...

Appreciate woman, you know the essences
Your smile is as genuine as expensive leather is

We've...

Brightly shone through the vicissitudes of cloudy weather
I cherish your kiss; I've been praised through your touch for and since forever

You...

Answer my call even if I think I'm asking too much
You're my man; I have always been your Lady, luck?

No, it's been written as such

We've...

Carried the weight proudly, we're not prideful
We knows our talent's power, we give minds an eyeful

You're...

My role model, you admire my role
You're my engineer, my seer, you know my every control

And...

With the ease of a summer's breeze, you've touched my soul
You're my destination, the very reason why I've walked these dark roads

I love you

I hear you and we join together in telepathic conversation... I say

I'm your man, you're my woman, and we're together
I'll follow your vibes; I'll follow your mind through whatever

And I'll break...

Through the walls of separation, swim through the river of doubt
I'll jump the valley of abandon; I'll swallow the pain of hurting shouts

You say...

I'll love you until I forget we're back in Egyptian pyramids and I'm senile
If all I saw were you and the Nile then I'd be content for infinite now's

We join in a simultaneous chant where we mentally state that...

I'll love you until the sands on shores disappear
Until transparent ideas represented in see-through dreams are no longer clear

I'll love you...

Until time stops telling and every tree starts leaving
Until fire doesn't burn for breaths of air, until logic has no reason

I'll love you...

Until virgin islands lose their fertility and souls have no entity
Until romantic Jamaican volcanoes no longer lava or until the question was never meant to be

We come to end our combined dissertation of emotion
Our attraction opens; it hugs us tightly as we stiffly comprehend this notion

Our glow... the aura of our spell is dimming and seems to be disappearing

Your tongue slowly returns back to your mouth
Our hands still holds the others face, my inner voices still shout

Whoa!!!

Our kiss... concludes

We drop our hands as we stare at each other
Our hearts are jumping and Time has finally kicked off the cover

You have you managed to seduce time to stop... It just now wakes back up

My mouth knows that anything besides your lips will be tasteless
Your beauty traps in my glare and makes me lightheaded and weightless

I question myself... will we ever fly away again?

Time speeds back up to one second per one second
I'm no longer dreaming, I truly realize now that you have flesh, you are a blessing

I grab and hold your hand... I speak my thoughts

"In every sense of the word with every sense of my being, I'm yours
Of that I'm sure, life can wreck me but I'll easily wash to your shores

Sink another kiss into my flowing attention and I'll surely float
With every silent prayer that I've sent up, you're everything for which I've hoped"

You smile and walk around me

You leave your purse on the table and walk out of the living room
The roasted chicken aroma livens and mixes with your perfume

Before I follow you out of the room I check the clock
Being skeptical of the time, I glance down to check my own watch

10:11pm

WHAT!!!

In my disbelief I manage to hear that you're calling me from the hallway
I still deny the hands on my wrist, this kiss seemed to last all day

Your voice still chills my body

I walk into the hallway but by that time you're in the kitchen
You're opening the oven and estimating how much time is left for the chicken

"How much longer do you think this chicken has?"
I shrug my shoulders, "15 minutes maybe, why do you ask?"

You close the oven door, turn around and then look at me
My optic nerve stimulates and my imagination reacts happily

My temperature is rising, the kitchen is warm indeed
The heat I'm feeling is from you though, you weaken my knees

You walk closer, check my watch as say that you're hungry
I restate that dinner should be ready soon but you say that you want me

We both smile

You rub your magnetic finger tips to my mouth until my lips sticks
A smile spreads to my face and once again my passion becomes wicked...

And your blazing glance ignites my hormones

Your touch brushes and lingers on my mouth as you leave
I rub my lips; I turn the oven to low and again slowly, I start to breathe

I inhale the rest of your scent that floats in the air

I walk from the kitchen back into the living room
Before I close the blinds I peer through the window to look at the moon

It's shining so bright... I'd be crazy not to fully appreciate tonight

I feel you rub my shoulders from behind, you un-tuck my shirt
You raise you hands under the cotton so that you can search

Can you feel the signature you left over my heart?

You rub my bare flesh and my muscles whisper "yes, yes, yes"
Your touch spans over my chest as your fingers leave my skin impressed

Ummph, you're an angelic masseuse

Your hands rotate around to my back as I spin to face you
I look into your eyes, "There is nothing in creation that could replace you"

I speak these words softly

"You're love and love is...

Like slow dancing in the warm sprinkles of summer's rain
Knowing that your partner will never aim to give you pain

I know you wouldn't and know that I won't

Love is that feeling... it's...

Like hearing your most uplifting song when you need it
It's like facing your fears with an attitude that won't allow you to be defeated

Your voice is my undeniable battle cry

Love is...

The most beautiful and inspiring feeling on Earth
It's the mystical potion for which every person thirsts

You are these things to me and I am these things to you

True Love, true love has similarities to a ghost
It's spoken of many but has been seen by fewer than most

Let's be the ghost of love's past, present, and future

You're...

The yin to my yang, the swoop in my swing
The gleam in my ring and you're that joyful song I sing

I've found you...

Now I'll cherish the circumstances and what I've went through
I'll do it again, with worse situations, since I know the end will present you

Only for you... and when...

I'm old and gray and can't remember each of our numerous loving phase
I'll still find joy in the lines that create your passionate and loving face

You are my poetry; you're every syllable of my speech
You're the audible expression when I speak; you're the one who brought me to
be

The whole world will know that fact

You've seen the best of me that hasn't always been visible and shown
Your love has been the under lying theme of my most appreciative poems

Since...

I noticed your proper curves activated my optic nerves
I knew that I had to keep the utmost sincerity to my verses and words"

You look into my eyes... I proceed... "Understand that...

If it's not on the bed then I'll never let you down
Only if we're hanging upside down on monkey bars do I want to see you frown

So know that...

The times, situation, nor the circumstances will change my love
You have my heart and I have yours, we won't fail at love

That's how it's been in the after life and that's how it'll stay after life

I'll walk with you until the roads of the universe are out of pavement
Until smell runs out of scent, until the glow stops being fluorescent

I'll give you all of me until...

I'm out of all of my breath

Until...

I'm alright with you because I'm all out of what's left

I'll give my all until...

Nothing's left, until Death gets tired of deaths

Until...

Each ear is deaf, until History blanks each noteworthy quest

I'll dream of you until...

My eyes are blind, my physical ones and the one in my mind

Until...

Upwards doesn't allude to a climb, until the jungles are out of vines

Until...

You come back to me without a spine

Until...

The shortest distance between two points isn't a straight line

I'll call to you until...

My throat is hoarse, until my hair isn't coarse

Until...

My hoarse voice becomes mute and burns like a torch

I'll fight my demons until...

Hell's no longer steaming, until the currents are no longer streaming

Until...

The truth lacks meaning and until holding on is done without clinging

I could be without fingers and I'll still come up with good points in why I support you
No neglecting, prematurely expecting, mis-directed, uneducated mission could ever abort you...

Ever... and...

Before my sex is dissected, I'll be twice man and double determined
I'll detoxify and D-con my inner vermin and purge myself through mental sermons

Stay with me

Stay with me until the winds cease to breeze, until Autumn finally leaves
Until dancing hearts don't need beats and there's no part of you in me

That'll be never... because...

Before I let you vanish and diminish...
I'll run on sentences bleeding periods allowing only the incomplete thoughts to be finished

There can't be me without thee, a we without He
I cherish every drop of blood bled that ever hit the street for this and you're all I need...

Because...

Even doused in sin I know we'll win, I'll give until I'm out of breath
Until I'm forced to be alright with you because I'm all out of what's left"

You open your mouth to speak but instead you pull my hand
You lead me to the stairs as I imagine we're transcending to higher lands

Each step of the stairs takes us up another notch, further in love
The walls along the steps disappear as we keep ascending above

We're traveling up a corridor; I see the light at the end of the tunnel
Our wide array of emotions will melt and pour out like the contents of a
passionate funnel

As we reach the second floor you turn to me and smile
"It's been one year and you've been so patient and have waited such a long while"

You press your finger to my lips to shush my whispers

You open my bedroom door, we shall bask in delight
I tip toe pass you and you close the door, everything feels so right

Will you make the son shine within the layers of the night?

I ease close to you and enjoy the proximity of our souls
We breathe in the same air; I can feel that you want to lose control

Your eyes are full of sultry desire, a volcanic type fire
I ask "How high are we going tonight?" you answer "Higher than the highest
higher"

Is that right?

You walk away from the door trailing your hand across my chest
Night's light is seeping into the room; our eyes capture sights of glimmering flesh

You glow just like an angel

I follow you around to the bed staying behind you closely
I align my arms around your waist; your warmth is what I've crave for mostly

We gaze at the moon and see the stars twinkling brightly
Oh, how much fun we've had sailing and navigating the night's seas

Tonight... we'll once again fly... this time... without our wings

You turn to me and rub my face as if for the first time
You examine my jaw line and lips; tonight will be our first time...

That we make love... at least this life time on Earth...

I can feel the wanting and the yearning of your flesh as I caress your arms
Our silent room is blaring with emotion; our intentions hear the exotic alarm

It's time... to awaken to a new day of pleasure

We agree without moving a muscle

And...

We agree without blinking an eye

We agree without the smallest hint of struggle

And...

We agree because every angel has already nodded from the skies

Yes... it is our time

Guidance is unspoken but we innately follow our soul's direction
We've always found ourselves together, we're drawn to the others affection

And... without accident...

You glance at the bed, hold my hands, and lower us to the sheets
Our sparks produce a fire of eroticism as we intend to birth true love within the
heat

You lean in and kiss me and all of the visions return
Every inch of your magnificence will receive my utmost concern

The room whirls...

Fast

Your tongue twirls...

Faster

I'm falling back in love...

Faster

The bite of your love bug...

Fast

Tonight we've experienced the sensations of an Eternal Kiss
Tonight, we'll experience the sensations of an Eternal Bliss

Because yes... it is definitely our time

About the Author

Stéphane Parker was born and raised in Detroit, Michigan. He's been writing short stories and poems since he was in the first grade. His family has always known him to possess a vivid imagination and merciless drive once he's decided on something. Stéphane's been writing online since 2004 once he was introduced to a social network called Xanga by Elizabeth Minisee. Since that time, he's written over 1,000 poems online for all to enjoy, critique and share. During the time he's been writing online, he's truly understood how passionate passages could change someone's life.

Upon receiving thousands of positive comments and remarks, he refocused his aim and became determined to publish a poetry book. After an extensive search for self-publishing companies, Stéphane found that none of these companies 'felt' right. So, for the past couple of years he's researched the steps of becoming a business owner. He started his own publishing company resulting from what he learned. Now he's the proud CEO and Regional President of Imperative Publishing, LLC, which will expand the vision that Stéphane has had since he was a small child; to tell stories that people will enjoy and remember. He may be emailed at ParkerRomance@ParkerRomance.com and followed @ParkerRomance.